ACTIVE
DUTY

ACTIVE DUTY
GAY MILITARY
EROTIC ROMANCE

EDITED BY
NEIL PLAKCY

CLEiS
PRESS

Published in the United States by Cleis Press, Inc., 2246 Sixth Street, Berkeley, California 94710.

Printed in the United States.
Cover design: Scott Idleman/Blink
Cover photograph: © David Vance
Fine art prints available at: www.davidvanceprints.com
Text design: Frank Wiedemann

First Edition.
10 9 8 7 6 5 4 3 2 1

Trade paper ISBN: 978-1-62778-031-5
E-book ISBN: 978-1-62778-048-3

Contents

INTRODUCTION

In the fourth century BC, Plato wrote in his *Symposium* that when soldiers loved each other, they would be particularly protective of each other in battle, and able to defeat much stronger armies. Whether their pairing led them into a sexual connection or not, there are stories of many soldier lovers, including Achilles and Patroclus, and Damon and Pythias.

However, antihomosexual sentiments have run rampant throughout history, affecting the military just as much as civilian society. Many Knights Templar were persecuted for same-sex affairs after the Crusades, and soldiers were whipped or discharged for "buggery" in the Napoleonic Wars and even in the American Revolution.

This policy was codified in the United States with the passage of Don't Ask, Don't Tell in 1993. It prohibited military personnel from discriminating against or harassing closeted homosexual service members or applicants, while barring openly gay persons from military service. It was not until the policy was repealed in 2011 that gay soldiers could be honest about who they love without fear of reprisal or dismissal.

The public displays of affection between soldiers and other men, the first same-sex service academy prom dates, and the first same-sex military weddings serve to illustrate something we have known all along—that gay men are strong, brave and resilient, the very characteristics that make a great soldier. Today, countries from Albania to Uruguay allow soldiers to serve regardless of sexual orientation, while there are still dozens with restrictions or ambiguous policies.

The stories in this collection celebrate the new freedom of American soldiers to love whomever they choose while still serving their country proudly. To quote President Harry S. Truman, "To you who answered the call of your country and served in its Armed Forces to bring about the total defeat of the enemy, I extend the heartfelt thanks of a grateful Nation."

Neil Plakcy
South Florida

WEEKEND LEAVE

Shane Allison

The night Tareek and I met, I had just gotten out of a ten-year friends with dick-sucking benefits with someone who I didn't realize until much later hadn't deserved me. The night I met Tareek, I had given Chris his walking papers, telling him that whatever it was, whatever we'd had was null and damn void. I wished him well and said my final good-bye. I was too through with his trifling, pussy-whipped ass. He was someone else's problem, and I was all too happy to kick him to the curb. As far as I was concerned, his bitch-on-wheels, baby's mama could have him. It was enough drama to make even a soap-opera diva say, "Dayuuummm!" I believe in karma like most people believe in God. And for Chris, it was a hood-rat bitch named Ikeara. But whatev. I'm over that white boy.

I wasn't about to go home and wallow. I was feeling too good about finally letting that muthafucka go after all those years. I wanted to celebrate, so I stopped off at my favorite watering hole, the Tomahawk, for a drink. I thought if I drank enough, it would wash away the years I wasted, the lies and bullshit. The

Tomahawk was littered with broke college students snacking on cheap appetizers and nursing on watered-down Coronas. Gawking at the bubble-headed buff boys was my favorite pastime. I had even hooked up with a few of them. College boys get horny as hell after a few beers.

I was on my second vodka cranberry, talking up Rob, this cute het bartender, when I felt a hand touch my arm.

"Is this seat taken?"

I turned to find this six-four, brawny, brown-skinned hunk of man standing behind me.

"It is now," I told him.

He cut me a smile as he slid in between me and the bar stool. My dick started to thicken when his thigh grazed mine.

Tareek was dressed in camouflage army garb, with a short haircut faded to the sides. I noticed his pretty light-brown eyes right away.

"What are you drinking tonight?" Rob asked him.

"Do ya'll have Guinness?"

"Absolutely, my friend," Rob said nicely. "What kind?"

"Do you have Red Stripe?"

"For sure."

"I'll have that."

Damn, he sounded masculine and sexy like he should be in a Jason Statham movie or something. He had pecs that were tight under all that brown and army-green camouflage. The last time I was in the presence of a man who was as fine as Tareek was...let me see, um...never. My palms were already starting to sweat and my dick was twitching like crazy in my shorts. I wanted nothing more than to reach over and squeeze one of his pecs, but my mama ain't raise no fool. He would probably mop the floor with my faggot ass if I so much as asked him to pass the beer nuts.

Rob popped the aluminum top off the bottle of Guinness.
"There you go, my friend," he said setting the cold bottle of
booze in front of him. I glanced over just as he brought the beer
to his juicy lips and took a swig. His beautiful throat pulsated
as I watched the beer wash down his gullet. *Jesus.*

I just sat there babysitting my vodka cranberry as Tareek
watched some kickboxing match that was playing out on the
fifty-inch TV that hung over the bar.

"Another VC, Rashawn?" Rob asked.

It was too early still to get shit-faced and I didn't want to
embarrass myself in front of this good-looking soldier who had
decided to sit next to me over all the other losers who were
saddled up to the bar.

"Let me try one of the...Red Stripes."

Rob glanced at me like he knew I was trying to impress
Tareek. He knew I couldn't stand the taste of Guinness.

"This shit taste like an ashtray," I once told him.

Rob popped off the top and set the bottle in front of me. I
was hoping that Tareek would take notice but he just kept those
pretty-ass eyes of his glued to the boob tube. I took a sip of Red
Stripe. I wanted to spit it out as soon as the nasty liquid hit my
palate. *Eww, that's gross,* I thought, but I played it off like I was
sipping on a birthday cake milkshake. I ran my thumb along the
front of the bottle. Condensation trickled off the hard, dark skin
of the glass onto my drink coaster like the pearls of sweat that
leaked from the roof of my armpits. I took several more gulps of
the beer in an effort to get up the balls to talk to Tareek.

"Are you coming or going?" I asked nervously.

Tareek looked over at me with those bedroom eyes and lips
the good Lord made for kissing.

"What's that?" he asked.

Within seconds, I had regretted asking him anything,

consciously beating myself up for being such a fucking dweeb.

"Are you about to go in or are you on leave?"

"Oh, I'm on leave, actually. Just for the weekend though, and then I return to base in North Carolina."

I almost couldn't believe that this fine-ass man was talking to me, that he was giving me the time of day.

"I'm Rashawn by the way," I said, with my hand extended.

"Tareek," he said, taking my hand firmly into his. "Nice to meet ya, man. So what do you do?"

"I'm a modeling agent."

"I would much prefer to do what you do. I'd run less of a risk of getting my ass shot off."

I didn't want to ask him questions about the war, and I didn't want to come off as being too nosey, so I changed the subject to something more lighthearted like college football, which I didn't know a thing about. I let Tareek do all the talking and hoped that whatever I had to offer made some semblance of sense.

That night we talked so late that Rob had to practically run us out of the bar.

"My bladder is about to explode," I said.

"You and me both," he laughed.

"You guys better make it quick 'cuz we're about to lock up," Rob said.

I trailed behind Tareek past booth seats and pool tables to the men's room in the rear of the bar. We stood in front of two urinals. The bathroom smelled like piss. I undid my fly and worked my dick out of the cotton panel of my draws, out past the copper teeth of my zipper. My dick was semi-hard, and a fast stream of piss splattered against the throat of the white porcelain.

The cruisy fag in me glanced over at Tareek's dick. He was packing eight, nine inches maybe, thick, with a milk chocolate hue to the shaft. I was literally salivating. *Damn, he's got a big dick.* I wanted to drop to my knees and veer his dick to my lips, the stream of piss and all, but like I said, my mama ain't raise no fool. My dick grew harder at the sight of Tareek's. I finished peeing before him and tucked my dick back inside my zipper. Tareek was done two seconds after.

Rob held the door open as we exited.

"All right, bruh, see you next time," he said, as he gave me dap. "Be safe over there, brother," he told Tareek.

I looked across the street at the clock at Tallahassee Capital Bank. It was five after three in the morning. I still didn't want to go home. I was off for three days from my job so it wasn't like I had to be on somebody's j-o-b the next day.

"Are you hungry? You want to get some breakfast?" Tareek asked.

The only thing I'd had to eat all day was a hot dog and some chips. I was too caught up in Chris's mess to eat, and I wasn't a big fan of what passed for food at the Tomahawk.

"Dog, you read my mind. I'm starving."

"Cool. There's a Waffle House a few blocks down the street if you feel like walking."

"Yeah, I could use the exercise."

"Is your car going to be okay here?" Tareek asked. "They ain't going to tow you or nothin' will they?"

"Naw, Rob is cool. He knows me."

I couldn't stop staring at Tareek's arms. I will do anything for a man in a tank top.

I could make out his abs thanks to the thin, ribbed cotton that hugged his torso. The mental pic of his candy bar-long dick was branded in my brain, and how he shook the last drops of piss off the meaty tip.

"So are you from here?"

"Born and raised and I hate it."

"Why?" Tareek grinned.

"There's not much to do. The bars suck, the club scene is like...nonexistent. Tallahassee has like *no* culture."

"I hear ya on that one. Where would you *like* to live?"

"I don't know. Atlanta, New York, maybe. I went to Fort Lauderdale once."

"Fort Laud is nice. I have family down there."

"I really don't care where I end up as long as I can get out of Tally."

When we got to the Waffle House, it was packed, which is always the scene after the bars and clubs let out. These coeds need scrambled eggs and hash browns to soak up all that cheap, watered-down beer.

"Damn, it's thick up in here."

It was so crazy people were filed out of the door like they were waiting to get food stamps or something.

"Let me ask the waitress how long it'll be before we can get seated," Tareek said.

He pulled this female dressed in a yolk-yellow dress and white apron off to the side and whispered in her ear like he was saying something pretty and sweet. She laughed. I watched as Tareek slipped a twenty spot in her hand.

"She's going to see what she can do."

"Do you know her?" I asked.

"Akaysha's brother is over in Basra. All of us grew up together in Pensacola."

Within a couple of minutes, Akaysha waved us over to a booth table she was clearing dishes from. I was already impressed within five hours of knowing Tareek.

We sat down as she laid two menus in front of us. She was mocha-toned with brown eyes and gorgeous features. Her hair was done up in a hairnet. Girlfriend was way too cute to be working in a diner. And a name as pretty as Akaysha didn't fit a waitress working in a greasy spoon. She had some supermodel, Naomi Campbell realness going on. Her manicure was on point, but I figured after slinging trays of dishes awhile, it wasn't going to stay that way.

"So have you heard from Jamaal?" Tareek asked.

"Got a letter from him last week. He's holding his own. He wants to go over and fight. He says they're over there just relaxing, getting some R&R and then they ship out to Afghanistan." Akaysha couldn't have looked more scared and worried. I thought she was going to faint right there across the table.

Tareek took her by the hand. "Jamaal is tough. He'll be okay. He's strong like his sister."

I could see tears welling up in her eyes. "It's just that...he's only nineteen, you know?"

"He's going to be fine. He'll have them fools over there breakdancing before you know it."

Akaysha grinned. "Yeah, you right."

"Have them doing the running man or something."

"Wow, that's pretty old school." Akaysha laughed.

"That makes me want to get up and do the cabbage patch up in here."

"Oh god, please don't," Akaysha pleaded.

"I agree," I said. "Please don't try to bring that dance back. Let it stay buried in the nineties."

The three of us burst out laughing. Akaysha took a pad and pen out of the pocket of her apron. "So what can I get ya'll to eat?"

We cracked open our menus. I was in a major mood for pancakes and patty sausage, so I already knew what I wanted. Tareek ordered first.

"Let me get the steak and eggs with a root beer."

Damn, steak and root beer for breakfast?

"Okay, it's going to be about ten minutes on that steak. Is that okay?"

"Yeah. We're not in any rush."

Akaysha scribbled down Tareek's order before she turned her attention to me.

"Let me try the blueberry pancakes with sausage and I'll have orange juice," I said.

Akaysha grinned as we handed her our menus. "Tareek, I'm glad you came through. I needed to laugh."

When he started rolling his arms, trying to do the cabbage patch while sitting down, Akaysha giggled.

"Boy, stop," she said, laughing. "I'll be back with y'all's food."

"That was one of the coolest things I have ever seen."

"What, my booth-seat cabbage-patch dancing?"

"The way you calmed her down like that. I could tell that she was upset about her brother."

"Well, you know what they say about laughter being the best medicine. Each other is all they have. Their grandmama raised them after their mama died from a drug overdose when they were kids. She wasn't about to let them become another statistic on the streets. Jamaal enlisted a few months after I did. I'm like the big brother he never had, I guess. He was always following me around, wanting to do everything I did."

"So he enlisted because you did?"

"Akaysha seems to think so, and she was pissed at me for a while thinking that I encouraged him to enlist in the army."

"And you didn't?"

"I didn't have a clue that Jamaal had enlisted until Akaysha wrote and told me. I just hope he's keeping his damn head down over there."

The Waffle House line was dying down. People either got seated or they left to go somewhere else to eat. The smell of bacon, sausage and fresh-brewed coffee permeated the diner. My stomach kept growling. Thankfully, Tareek couldn't hear how hungry I was with all of the talking from the other tables.

"So can I ask you something? How does your girlfriend feel about you going to Iraq?"

"Not sure. I don't have one."

Yes!

"What about you? Are you seeing anyone?" Tareek asked.

"I just got out of a bad relationship. And I mean *just* got out of one like seven hours ago."

"Sorry to hear that."

"I'm not. He was a shit chicken."

"A shit chicken?" Tareek laughed.

Akaysha sauntered toward our table with a tray of food. "Here, let me help you," I said.

Akaysha handed me a plate of blueberry pancakes with four sausage patties on the side and two butters. Tareek's T-bone steak was sizzling on the plate with a side of scrambled eggs. She sat the large glasses of orange juice and root beer on the table next to silverware cocooned tightly in napkins.

"Can I get ya'll anything else?"

"I think we're good here, baby girl," Tareek said.

Akaysha had a smile that could make the meanest of men purr. "All right, just wave if you need me."

"This looks good," Tareek said.

"She needs to be on the cover of a magazine somewhere."

"Who? Akaysha?"

"God, yes. She's gorgeous."

"People tell her that all the time, but she doesn't ever take them seriously."

"I would love to get her in the studio, take a few shots of her. The modeling industry could use more sisters."

"I don't know, but you can try." We unfurled silverware out of our napkins.

Armed with a steak knife, Tareek cut into his meat as I drowned my blueberry pancakes in syrup. "Mmm…this is a pretty good steak. You want a bite?"

Tareek had no idea how badly I wanted a taste of his *meat*. "It looks good. I should have ordered that instead."

Tareek ran a piece of the beef in steak sauce with his fork. "Here, try it," he said, leaning across the table.

I wrapped my mouth around the savory morsel of meat and then sucked it from the tip of his fork.

"How is it?"

"Mmm…that is good."

The last time I was fed from someone's plate, I was five. I found his maneuver kind of romantic. If I hadn't known any better, I would have thought I was falling for Tareek. I still didn't know if he was *one of the children* yet.

The next time she stopped by our table, I told Akaysha that I was a modeling scout. She thought I was bullshitting until I gave her one of my cards. I told her to come by the office Monday morning.

"That face oughta be on the cover of *Vogue*," I told her.

She laughed and tucked my business card into her apron pocket.

"I'm serious. Come by. My friend Bryan Brown would love to take some shots of you."

"Oh my god, I know him. He's one of the best photographers in Tallahassee."

"Yes, and I want you to come meet him."

"Okay, I'll do that."

When Tareek took out his wallet to pay for our meal, Akaysha said, "It's on the house."

Tareek insisted on leaving her a twenty-dollar tip. He gave Akaysha a kiss on the cheek followed by a hug before we left. "You keep in touch and be safe over there," she said.

It was ten after six when we got back to my car in the parking lot of the bar. "Thank you for breakfast," I said.

"Thank you for the company."

I kept my hands nervously in my pockets.

"Now can I ask you something?" Tareek said.

"Anything."

"Can I kiss you?"

I don't know if my heart was thumping crazy from the walk back to the bar or from the prospect of being kissed by this gorgeous Adonis of a man. My suspicions had been confirmed. Tareek was gay. I wanted to say, "Hell yeah you can kiss me," but I kept cool.

"Okay."

I didn't care who was around or who might see. I wasn't going to pass up the opportunity to be kissed by Tareek. I leaned against the door of my Cadillac Escalade as he leaned into me. His lips were warm and supple against mine. I thought about sticking my tongue in his mouth, but I didn't want to come off fresh on what I guessed was our first date. When I felt his arms around my waist, I thought I was going to melt. *Please don't let me be dreaming this shit.*

"That was nice. You're a good kisser," he said.

"Um...you too."

My dick was so hard in my shorts you would have thought I had overdosed on Viagra.

"You like basketball?" Tareek asked.

"I've watched a few games."

"The Seminoles are playing Wake Forest tomorrow night. You wanna go?"

"Sounds like fun, yeah, sure."

We exchanged phone numbers. I gave Tareek the address of my apartment.

"The game starts at seven thirty, so I'll pick you up at seven."

The minute I got home that night, I grabbed a bottle of lotion and some tissues and jacked my dick as I thought of Tareek deep-dicking me in the ass.

We had dinner the following night at Po' Boys and then went back to his aunt's house, as she was conveniently in Biloxi over the weekend. We cuddled on her flower-printed sofa, sliding hands under shirts and between each other's legs, feeling at each other's brick-hard dicks.

Tareek kissed me, sliding his tongue in my mouth, past my lips. We kissed each other hard. When I lay on top of him, I felt his dick sticking warm against my thigh. Tareek's tongue tasted sweet like candy.

"Let's take this to the bedroom."

Tareek and I kissed, peeling each other out of our shirts as we walked lip-locked to the room he was staying in. Afrocentric portraits hung on each wall. There was a chest of drawers in front of one of the bedroom windows that were hung with sheer, white curtains and a dresser with tiny blue-and-white figurines that matched the color scheme of the bedroom. It definitely showed a woman's touch. Items like bottles of cologne, a brush and other miscellaneous male items were strewn along the dresser. A colorful assortment of fake carnations and a clock radio sat on one nightstand while a phone and a couple of crystal candy jars sat on the left side of the bed. It reeked of potpourri. There were shirts and jeans neatly folded in a white rocking chair in one corner of the room. Tareek's dog tags hung around the neck of one of the bedposts. We fell onto the king-sized bed that was decorated with fat pillows and a flower-printed bedspread.

Tareek undid the buckle of my belt and the clasp of my jeans. He tore my boots from my feet, throwing them to the floor before he pulled off my jeans. Being that I wasn't in the best of shape, I was nervous about him seeing me naked. Tareek didn't seem to mind. His fingers tickled as they grazed delicately against my thigh. My dick popped free like a jack-in-the-box when he pulled my draws past my waist, around my booty and down to my feet.

I stopped him when he started to undress himself. "Here, let me." Tareek dropped his arms to the side and let me do the honors. He kicked off his boots as I pulled his tan camouflage uniform pants down his muscle-bound legs. The bulge in the tent of his boxers caused me to salivate. I had been anxious to get my lips around his meat since the night before in the bathroom at the Tomahawk. I hooked my fingers over the waistband of his underwear, easing them off his milk-chocolate skin. My cut seven-incher had nothing on his ten-inch appendage that literally banged against my chin.

"Damn, T."

"We both know you can handle my dick," he said.

"I've wanted to do this since the bathroom."

"I figured you did. I saw you checking out my dick."

I tongued the head, licking precum from the teardrop spout before I enveloped the head with my mouth. He slid along my lips like a dream.

"Turn over for me. I want you to feel me inside you."

I did what Tareek wanted. There was a bottle of lotion on

the dresser sitting next to a blue and white porcelain pig. Tareek slathered it along his dick. He smeared himself on top of me. Black skin kissing black skin. I felt his dick pressing into the ditch of my ass, the tips of his fingers traipsing along my nips.

Tareek pushed until I felt his bulbous crown slip in past my asshole.

"You okay?" Tareek asked, as he started to thrust.

"Fuck, this feels good."

"Yeah, you like me inside you?"

"Don't stop."

I watched Tareek's dick sliding in my ass reflected in the dresser mirror. He pinned my hands to the pillows as he fucked me.

"Damn, this some good ass."

"And it's all yours," I told him as he kissed me along the nape of my neck. Tareek was a man who knew his way around a man's ass, who knew all the right buttons to push.

"Turn over."

Tareek flipped me over on my side. He tweaked my nips as he pulled me into his dick.

"Don't stop. Keep fucking me," I pleaded.

Tareek had me. This soldier was a pro at deep-dicking booty.

He toyed with my balls, jacking my piece from the front while fucking me from the back.

"I want you to come with me," Tareek said.

"Fuck yeah."

Our breathing was heavy. His pumps of my dick were in sync with his thrusts.

"I'm about to nut. Cum with me," Tareek pleaded, as he pumped my dick crazy.

"Fuck me, Tareek!"

"Shit yeah!"

I couldn't hold out. "I'm 'bout to cum, damn!"

Within seconds, jets of white spurted from my spout onto his aunt's flower-printed bedsheet. The woman would probably keel over with a heart attack if she saw me and her nephew butt-ass naked in her bed. My cum oozed over Tareek's fingers. He pulled out of my booty and shot warm strings of nut. Tareek held me close as we came together in sloppy-wet French kissing.

"That was amazing."

"You're amazing," I said.

That night we fell asleep in each other's arms. I felt Tareek's soft dick against my booty as we spooned. There was nowhere else I wanted to be.

We spent the whole weekend together. Sunday was his last day before he had to leave, so we had brunch and went to a movie. "What time does your bus leave for North Carolina tomorrow?" I asked, as we walked out of the movie theater.

"Six a.m."

"Can I drive you to the bus station?"

"Are you sure?"

"We can get breakfast tomorrow before we go. I want to give you a proper sendoff."

I hated the idea of him leaving but I understood why. It was a little after four in the morning when we got to the Waffle House. Tareek looked so handsome in his uniform. Akaysha wasn't working. This time we both ordered the steak and eggs. We didn't talk much. I didn't want Tareek to leave, but I didn't tell him that.

"It might rain today," I said.

Tareek stared out of the tinted window of the diner. "Looks like it."

We got to the bus station twenty minutes before Tareek's bus departed for North Carolina. I struggled to keep from crying.

"Call me when you can. Write, email, something to let me know that you're okay."

"Will you do me a favor?"

"Anything."

"Look out for Akaysha for me. She doesn't have anyone else."

"I promise."

Tareek and I hugged. "Come back to me. That's a fuckin' order."

"Yes, sir," he grinned.

As the bus pulled out of the terminal, I mouthed to Tareek. *I love you.*

He pressed his hand to the glass. *I love you, too.*

It wasn't until I got in the car that I cried. Not because Tareek was gone, but because I was in love.

LETTER FROM HOME

Jay Starre

P rivate Abe Mason offered fellow private Keith Smith a letter and lingered while he opened it, expecting his pal to share some of the news from home. Their base in Georgia was far from Abe's home in New York City and Keith's in Tulsa, Oklahoma. They were a long way from their families and friends.

"Peter is splitting up with me. Seems like he's found someone else who's got a hotter ass than mine," Keith said with a slight grin.

That shy smile was a real turn-on for the dark-skinned private who hovered over him. Everything about the freckle-faced soldier was a turn-on, even the way he took the bad news with a bit of humor.

"That sucks. He sounds like a bastard. Good riddance, I say."

"Naw. He's not a bastard at all. He's just kind of flaky. I wouldn't be surprised if he changes his mind a month from now."

"Would you take him back?"

"Not likely. Lesson learned, I reckon."

And that was all he said about it, but Abe could tell he was really down. "Come on, bud. Let's go for a ride. We have a couple of hours and no one's going to argue if we take the jeep out for a little reconnaissance practice in the hills."

Keith readily agreed, obviously eager to get some air—and maybe take his mind off that unwelcome letter. The two had become fast friends from the first day of basic training, and it was hardly unusual for them to take off together whenever the opportunity arose. Abe was training as a driver in the motor pool, and it was easy enough to get permission to take one of the vehicles out.

Although Keith was the quiet one, he had been the one to admit he was gay when they met. When Abe asked if he had a girlfriend back home, the green-eyed recruit had confided without the slightest shame that he had a boyfriend back in Oklahoma. Abe had quickly revealed he was gay too. Neither would have been able to do that without great risk only a few months earlier with the military's old antigay policy still in effect.

Their conversation on the way out of the base into the nearby hills was typical of their usual talks. Even with the roar of the jeep's engine and the creaking and shaking of its chassis as they bumped their way over the dirt track, Abe could be heard. He had a deep voice, very melodic and very sexy. He had no need to shout or raise it, as the deep timbre could be heard even from far away, almost like an elephant's throaty rumble. Keith, though, was not only shy but also had a soft prairie drawl and often had to repeat himself.

At first they didn't mention the letter, nor did they mention their imminent deployment to Afghanistan. Instead they talked about every other subject under the sun. Abe was a bit of a know-it-all while fortunately Keith was interested in just about any topic his garrulous buddy touched on.

Finally, though, Keith broached the subject on both of their minds. "We're going off to the battlefield in less than a week. Heck, now that Peter's dumped my sorry ass I won't have anyone back home to worry about me. Other than Grandma Murphy."

Abe instinctively reached over and placed a hand on his pal's broad shoulder and squeezed. "Fuck that asshole. You got Grandma rooting for you anyhow...and you've always got me."

"Thanks, Abe. But it does kind of suck. Not to be a baby about it, but I had sort of counted on Peter back home thinking about me while I was off fighting, you know, someone who wouldn't forget about me no matter how far away I was. All that romantic stuff."

"I won't forget about you, and I'll be right there by your side. Like now."

Keith had been looking at the dense Georgia woods lining the road as he spoke, but now dared to turn to his friend and smile his appreciation. There were tears in his eyes.

"Hell, buddy! There's no use in letting it get to you. How about if we park somewhere and fuck our miseries away? Now that you don't have a boyfriend anymore, I can hit on you without feeling like a home-wrecking asshole."

Keith burst out laughing, then squealed with surprise and delight when Abe's hand on his shoulder suddenly plunged into his lap and squeezed his crotch. "Don't tease me, Abe! I've seen your cock, and I have to admit I've entertained a few fantasies about it!"

"You have? Like what? A little sucking, a little fucking? A little of both? A lot of both?"

Keith answered by thrusting his own hand into Abe's lap and groping. He discovered a throbbing lump under the army khakis and dared to give it a good squeeze too.

"We're pulling over," Abe shouted as they groped each other and whooped with laughter.

He was a good driver. Even with one hand massaging Keith's cock, and his buddy's hand massaging his own swelling meat, he managed to pull off the dirt road and park the jeep under the sweeping branches of an oak tree that hid them from any view from the air. Rigorous training had taught them that much, along with the need for shade on the sunny afternoon.

The moment the jeep screeched to a halt they went at it. Still laughing, Keith scrambled up to kneel in the passenger seat while Abe pulled himself up to stand above him in the driver's seat. In the dappled shade, Abe's sepia-brown skin glowed and his big dark eyes seemed to glitter. He smiled and winked as he unzipped his fly, then fished out his giant black dick. And it was a giant.

Already stiff from just contemplating the outcome of their heart-to-heart conversation during the ride out there, Abe's meat rose up in a tower of quivering girth. Long and fat and lined with pulsing veins, it was more than a mouthful, but Keith didn't even hesitate.

Bowed red lips parted and a broad tongue came out to lap at the flared crown bobbing in the private's face. His green eyes were intent on the target before him and he swooped in to surround the dark cockhead with those plump lips. He began stroking it with his tongue while slowly swallowing up inch after inch of the lengthy shaft.

Abe's hefty thighs shook as he gasped aloud. Staring down at the fair-haired private gurgling over his cock, he could hardly believe his good fortune. The dude was a muscular hunk and

a real sweetheart too! He felt bad that things hadn't gone well
with Keith and his boyfriend, but it sure was working out for
him. The wet suction engulfing his stiff meat had him shuddering from head to toe, and the sight of the private's round ass
rearing backward from his slim waist only increased his trembling excitement.

He had to feel that butt. He'd been checking it out since their
training started and now there was the distinct possibility it
could be his for the taking! He leaned over and reached for it
with both hands. Of course that action drove his cock deeper
into Keith's busy mouth but the private took it with ease. As
those big paws gripped his asscheeks, the blond tore open his
khakis and shoved them down to his knees.

Abe grinned wickedly as he yanked down on Keith's olive-
green boxers and completed the strip job. "Hell yeah! What a
sweet damn ass! Lily white and smooth as silk. Fuck! Spread
your legs for me, Private!"

The growled words in that deep voice spiked with nasty
dirty talk had Keith scrambling to obey his buddy's demand.
He shoved his pants and skivvies farther down until they
tangled in his boots. He spread his knees as far apart as
possible to splay wide and offer up a tempting view of his deep
white asscrack.

The dark-skinned soldier hovering above laughed appre-
ciatively as he gripped the full cheeks and spread them farther
apart. He found himself staring at a pouting flushed hole in the
center of that pale valley. The fingers of one hand slid into the
open crack and down to that tempting slot. He grinned as he
found it and began to stroke the wrinkled rim.

Keith slobbered and gulped as he reared back into those
teasing fingertips. His obvious pleasure intensified Abe's own
desires. He ran his fingers all over the rim and entrance and was

delighted to see the hole push outward, then clench, then gape apart. Bent over with his pal's face buried in his crotch, Abe was perfectly positioned to open his mouth and spit down into the splayed buttcrack.

"Hell yeah! Sweet," he muttered as he began to rub the slippery goo all over the quivering hole.

Keith's broad shoulders were beautifully outlined by his olive-green T-shirt while his narrow waist emphasized the swell of his perky buttcheeks. One of Abe's brown hands clasped a white cheek while the other probed the crack. The contrast of brown on white was sharp, especially where the darker fingertips played with the spit-coated pink hole.

The kneeling soldier's ass wriggled and jerked as those fingertips began to work the spit into the quaking center of his hole, then slowly slithered past the defending ring of snapping muscle. Abe spit on it again, and again, then worked the gooey lube deep into his buddy's hot ass-channel.

The brown index finger disappeared up the pink hole. Keith moaned deep in his chest and heaved backward toward the deep insertion, then jerked all over as that buried finger twisted inside him and jabbed at his prostate. More spit landed on his open crack and a second finger eased its way into him.

There was spit everywhere as Abe continued to hawk down gobs of it into Keith's crack and the fair-haired soldier on his knees slurped noisily around the huge dick in his mouth. More spit dribbled from his pursed red lips, glistening on his chin and foaming over the dark shaft sliding in and out of it.

Feeling the warm innards and clinging asslips surrounding his pair of buried fingers had Abe thinking of what else he could do to that obviously hungry hole. It was still tight, even with two big fingers stretching it from the inside, so he knew he'd have to work on it before his monster dick could breach it.

He knew what would work. First he would lather it up good with more spit and dig deep with those probing fingers. Then he'd eat it out!

The brown fingers pushed in and out, spit bubbling around the puckered asslips, then twisted, stabbed and pulled on the rim from the inside before finally slithering out. The hole gaped open momentarily before clamping down again with spit dribbling from the snapping center.

Keith's pale ass wriggled all the while then reared upward as the fingers slipped out of him. He was ready for the next stage of Abe's assault. "Get up and lean over the windshield," Abe ordered. "Get out of those pants too. I want you spread wide open."

The kneeling private pulled out the dark cock buried in his throat and snorted for air. The big thing bobbed in the air in front of him, shiny with his spit and flushed a deep purple. He briefly contemplated how it would feel shoved in his ass, which is what Abe certainly had planned. It would be interesting.

"I hope you've got some kind of lube besides my spit and yours, Abe. This thing is big."

The understatement uttered in that gentle drawl had Abe's cock jerking wildly. He smiled as he moved his hands to grip Keith under the armpits and lift him. The dude was heavy—solid muscle from head to toe. The only soft spot on his body was that spit-gobbed hole deep down in the smooth crack.

"There's something in the glove box that'll work. Get stripped, spread your legs and don't worry about it."

"That's what they all say," Keith joked.

Abe laughed as he dropped his own pants and underwear and kicked them off over his boots. He knelt in the backseat while his buddy completed his own stripping and placed a boot on each of the bucket seats, then leaned over the windshield as he'd been told.

"How's that? Private Smith's ass is ready for service, sir," he joked.

"Yum! Time for a tongue-lashing, Private," Abe replied as he reached out and gripped the full cheeks with his hands and spread them even wider.

The spit-wet hole was pink and moist and already pushing outward in anticipation of his attack. A pair of pink balls hung down between the muscular thighs but the soldier's cock was pointing sky-high and not readily visible from behind.

As Abe buried his face in the open crack he reached around with one hand and found that rearing boner. He began to pump it slowly as his tongue swiped over the twitching hole and his lips grazed the rim.

Now was the time to really loosen up the slot for what would come next. A good licking and sucking always worked, in his experience. He lapped at the entrance with his broad tongue and was pleased when it yawned open. That was a good sign, considering his cock was bigger than most and would test the limits of any hole it attempted to breach.

He used one hand to stroke Keith's stiff cock while he used the other to squeeze and massage the solid buttcheeks surrounding his buried face. The pale ass was smooth all over and incredibly firm, although the cheeks quivered and jerked as his tongue tickled the pink entrance to the soldier's ass-channel.

His own cock soared upward and jerked in sympathy. He loved to eat ass, and now he launched a slobbering, wet attack that had Keith crying out with groaning pleasure, but his cock was far too stiff and eager for him to deny it for long.

Offering a final lap of big tongue along his pal's deep crack, he rose to his feet then reached around the bent-over soldier to open up the glove box. He'd planted a bottle of baby oil there when they left base earlier and was glad he'd been so optimistic! Now it would be useful.

He squirted a stream of the slippery liquid over his rearing boner then planted it between his pal's white asscheeks. The dark tool glistened against the pale flesh, twitching and leaking. He was so excited he desperately wanted to ram it deep into that sweet ass. But he didn't.

Now was the time for a little tenderness, he figured. He had what he craved, Keith's gorgeous body bent over the jeep's windshield and squirming back against him with obvious need, but there was more.

He really, really liked the sweet Oklahoma stud. He wanted more than a quick and exciting fuck. Time to show him that! He rubbed the huge length of his dark cock in that deep crack and leaned over to place his lips on the soldier's neck. He kissed him tenderly as he slowly pumped Keith's crack with his slippery cock.

He fucked the crack for a few delicious minutes, teasing the wriggling soldier with the length and girth of his hot rod before finally planting the dark knob directly on the trembling entrance. He slowly pushed as Keith turned his head and their lips met.

They kissed deeply as that giant cockhead slithered beyond the twitching asslips and slowly burrowed home. Abe's big hands roamed all over Keith's torso and crotch as he pumped in and out in a steady grind, slow but deep, then faster and faster as they both got caught up in the steamy pleasure of cock massaging hole and the irresistible need for orgasm.

Keith groaned around Abe's tongue in his mouth as he gripped the windshield and drove back against the giant tool invading him from behind. His greed for all that stiff heat up his ass overwhelmed all of Abe's patient regard. He fucked himself over the giant cock, groaning and humping and slobbering until his own cock erupted in a spray of gooey spunk all over that same windshield.

Abe felt his buddy's asshole convulse around his buried cock as Keith spewed. He'd managed to hold back while the muscular soldier rode his cock with his steamy slot, but now he finally gave in to the boiling need for release. He yanked his cock out and let fly. A geyser of spooge coated Keith's wriggling white ass.

They remained locked together for a few more minutes as they caught their breath and allowed their pounding hearts to return to a more normal pace. It was Abe who spoke first.

"I gotta ask you something, Keith. Did you have the hots for me before you got that letter from home?"

"What do you think? Of course. But I wouldn't want to cheat on my boyfriend."

"So does that mean you're all mine now?"

"Appears so."

It was a few months later when the proof of that quiet statement became all too clear. The day had been a violent one. The armored carrier Abe drove struck an IED and was blasted off the Afghanistan highway into a roadside ditch. It wasn't the first time his vehicle had been unfortunate enough to hit a roadside bomb and Abe managed to control their crash to a certain extent. Dazed, he scrambled out to check on the men in the back.

"Damn, you're okay," he cried out with relief, as he helped Keith from the wreckage.

They hugged briefly but fiercely before pulling the rest of the men to safety.

That night back at their base, the two managed to catch a rare moment of privacy behind the mess hall in the darkness of a starry Afghan night. They kissed passionately, glad to be alive and glad to be in each other's arms. Neither could resist the urge to fuck, and with their dusty khakis around their knees, Abe tenderly and deeply plowed his pal's pale white ass with his fat black cock.

While they fucked in the starry darkness, Keith turned his head to whisper in his soldier-lover's ear. "I got a letter from home today. Seems Peter wants me back after all."

Abe hardly missed a stroke, sliding his immense meat in and out of Keith's hot hole slowly and steadily. "What are you going to tell him?"

"What do you think? I'm going to tell him 'Sorry, pal. I got myself someone with a much bigger cock,'" he teased.

Abe made sure to slide his dick all the way home, burying it to the balls and turning Keith's snicker into a deep groan.

With the two soldiers happily grinding and groaning in heated lust, the dangers around them seemed far, far away that night. Home, for now, seemed as close as each other's arms.

DO ASK,
DO TELL

Julian Mark

S kin it back and squeeze the knob," Sergeant Baker ordered.

Welcome to Monday morning short-arm inspection, a ritual to ensure that none of the troops had dipped their wicks into anything contagious over the weekend. Sergeant Billy Baker, our personal dick inspector, roused us with a shrill whistle at five-fucking-A.M. We stumbled out of our cots, uppers and lowers, and stood tall in a variety of undergear that would gladden the heart of Calvin Klein. To wit: boxers, briefs, boxer-briefs and come-fuck-me ball-huggers.

"Drop your drawers," was the sergeant's next command, which was not necessary because after three months of basic training we astute recruits knew the drill. As the boys complied I always wanted to shout, "HOLD YOUR HAT AND HALLE-LUJAH, PAPA'S GONNA SHOW IT TO YOU." However, being a legally gay PFC, as I now was, did not give me the right to break into song at the drop of a guy's jockey shorts nor, for that matter, the right to drop to my knees.

We were a dozen tent mates residing under a canvas tarp over a concrete slab. The accommodations gave new meaning to the word *sparse*. The tent held six double-decker cots, three on either side of the twelve-by-twenty concrete floor, each cot assigned a footlocker. This Monday-morning display of manly pulchritude often reminded me of the West Point dictum, "You can measure a man's courage by the length of his foreskin."

Alas, there was only one courageous man among our snipped dozen.

This was Julio Zapata, who everyone mistakenly called Julie. Julio was a cross between Fernando Lamas, Ricardo Montalban and Adonis. To watch Julio skin it back was like contemplating a vegetarian's dinner treat. Mushroom head, cucumber and two kiwis. My jack-off dream was to skin Julio back with my lips while Sergeant Baker waited his turn. Yes, I'm assuming Sergeant Baker was a courageous man, however I never actually saw proof as required by West Point dick authorities. The sergeant never joined his charges on piss break in the field. Was he part camel?

Jacking off was another activity being legal did not address, albeit being legal did not figure into the dilemma. Gay, straight, bi or trans, the American boy's first affair is with his fist, to which he remains true till the Grim Reaper brings down the curtain. To quell our raging hormones and the urge to fuck with a partner, the ever-helpful Sergeant Baker recommended going into a corner to jack off. Cohabitating in our tent was obviously a no-no regardless of one's legality.

Do you get the feeling that being legally gay in the army is not much different from being illegal? In fact, it's rumored that closeted GI's have more fun (i.e., sex) than those who wave the rainbow flag. Straight guys with hard pricks and no women are reluctant to make a gay buddy know they are not averse to a good blow job. To court a gay is to be gay, or so many would deduce. But a straight could cozy up to a "suspect" and get his rocks off to the satisfaction of all concerned without the straight being compromised. Don't ask about it, don't tell about it, just do it.

I've never seen any of the troops jacking off in a corner. If I did, I would join the bugger and perhaps initiate a twelve-man circle jerk. Jacking off in a double-decker cot would be as unobtrusive as dancing the twist (shake, rattle and roll), thereby depriving your bunkmate of a good night's sleep. Also, where do you deposit the cum if you don't have a willing receptacle? A condom? Then you have to get rid of the loaded rubber. A sock? It would be rather sticky in the morning. A towel? You can't say nighty-night to your tent mates, then take a towel to bed. To let yourself cum on the sheets results in pecker tracks, signs of which the troops are constantly on the lookout for.

Wet dreams can also result in pecker tracks; however, pecker-track inspectors know a wet-dream stain from a jack-off stain. In a wet dream the cum seeps out slowly, forming a spot about the size of a quarter. Jacking off lets loose a spray that anoints a huge area including the guy's chest, belly and even his chin where an agile tongue can lick it off, and this ends up staining a large area of the sheet.

The on-base USO is a refuge to troops in need of a place to defecate and masturbate without an audience. Ours had a latrine that boasted six stalls and a gay facilitator who organized bingo games, family visits, emergency leaves, Scrabble competitions and, so I learned, gang bangs. His name was Ralph. He was about fifty, slim, with graying hair, and from the outline of the long pecker in his chinos I would say he dressed to the left.

Ralph and I recognized each other as soul mates from the time of my first visit to the USO facility. Knowing I didn't play bingo or Scrabble he asked me if I had come for a game of pool, the question spoken with a nod toward the sergeant who was at the pool table, playing solo. I shook my head, hefted the bulge in my crotch and headed for the latrine. "Take the last stall," Ralph advised me as I went for the much pent-up release.

I took the last stall because I had learned to follow orders as befits a lowly PFC, and I didn't bolt the door because I suspected Ralph had it in mind to peek in or perhaps join me for a community wank. I dropped my pants and shorts, and sat and fisted my cock, which was already stiff with anticipation. I gave my balls a playful rub and drew precum after two strokes. Then the door opened a crack and a head appeared. It wasn't Ralph. It was the sergeant.

"I'm looking to get sucked off," he announced.

"Well, Sergeant, you've come to the right place."

He came in, closed the door and dropped his pants and jockeys. His prick was semi-hard, thick and displayed a helmet-shaped head with a drop of man juice at the piss-slit. His man bush was abundant and ran up his heaving belly. His balls were huge low hangers which I cupped as he shoved his cock toward my lips. "Kiss it, pal."

I tongued the piss-slit and got a mixture of salty cum and the unmistakable taste of man piss. He must have taken a leak before coming to the stall. I was so hot my own cum juice was flowing like water from a leaky faucet. The sergeant put his hand on my head and pushed me onto his cock. I lapped up the big head like a kid with a lollypop, the ones we called all-day suckers. I began to caress his prick with my lips and tongue. Holding my head he fucked my face with slow, circular motions, aiming for my tonsils. It had been a long time since I'd had a taste of cock, and I was lapping it up like a starved puppy.

I put my arms around my sergeant to grasp his ass and—

holy shit, I was touching not ass but skin in need of a shave. It was Ralph, who had squeezed into our stall and was licking the sergeant's ass. From the moans the sarge was sighing I figured Ralph was giving him an in-depth rim job.

"I'm the meat of the sandwich," the sergeant quipped as he shoved his cock in my mouth and his A-hole onto Ralph's tongue. The happy noncom was wiggling as best he could in our tight quarters. "Okay, men, let's share the goodies." With that the sarge disengaged his sucker and licker, then turned around as best he could with his pants and jockeys around his ankles until I faced his ass and Ralph got the prick with the helmet head and low hangers.

I went right to work. Ralph had licked the sarge clean but I continued to polish the apple, so to speak. I reached between the sergeant's legs and tickled his balls and Ralph's chin. Then I dipped a finger in my abundant precum and shoved it up the sergeant's back door. He jumped which must have rammed his cock down Ralph's throat. "You fucking me?" he yelled.

"Just a finger-fuck, Sarge."

"Had a major that liked to finger-fuck me. Got so loose he could put two fingers up my poop hole."

"Did he lick his fingers?" I wanted to know.

"Fuck, no. He made me lick them. Rank has its privileges."

The sergeant backed into me (remember, I was sitting on the toilet to give Ralph room to stand up.) "He's putting a raincoat on me," the sarge informed me. (A raincoat, for you civilian readers, is a condom and if dicky has a hood always skin it back before putting on his raincoat; the army's complimentary condoms came with these instructions.)

Ralph turned and pressed his face against the closed door, giving sarge clear access to Ralph's poop tube, a territory the sarge seemed to know very well because he buckled his knees a few inches, aimed his helmeted soldier at the mark and entered the fort without a moment's hesitation. Ralph moaned, the sergeant moaned and I tongued the sarge as the sarge fucked the USO facilitator. We were a fucking team. (Excuse the pun.)

Sarge was the first to drop his load, and his moans and spasmodic shivers told his mates it was a rapture supreme. I was next, spraying the sarge's ass with my man cum. My rapture had me licking my cum and tonguing it up Sarge's bumhole. Ralph brought himself off with his fist, rendering the stall aromatic with the scent of jism and man sweat. Exhausted, we untangled ourselves slowly, like sardines vying for fin room.

The sarge's condom hung low with his load of thick, white boy juice. The ever-helpful facilitator bent to inch it off Sarge's cock, *with his lips.* I caught a glimpse of Ralph's cock; uncut with the foreskin not able to completely clear the cockhead. A tasty delight for many a discriminating gourmand.

Ralph peeped out to make sure there was no one about to see him coming out of the stall. He told us he would return with a wet towel, of which we were in much need. With our pants and shorts still around our ankles, Sarge and I took a warm piss pas de deux. Sarge fingered my butt and got in a few inches as we made water. "I want to fuck you next time," he told me.

"Would you kiss me first?" I asked.

He shook the last drops of piss off his dick and said. "Kiss this, buddy."

Was he asking me or telling me?

We went to the rifle range for target practice once a week. How we got there is significant to my tale of sex in the new Army, which was not flagrant but certainly performed with more joie de vivre than in the days of Don't Ask, Don't Tell, when everyone asked and no one told.

The motor pool, staffed by men with much brawn and big baskets, provided the transportation, a covered wagon with a row of benches flanking a wood flatbed and attached to a cab. We troops were ushered in over the tailgate like biped cattle going to the slaughter. The first men in filled the benches from rear to front. The following men had to stand, filling the space between the benches from rear to front.

The first man in, of course, got the first bench seat in the rear of the wagon. This was Bobby Benson, the company clerk. Company clerks are exempt from all physical basic training, except rifle practice, a perk of being a computer wiz. The army that used to travel on its stomach now travels via the computer.

I was the first standee to jump the tailgate and head for the rear of the wagon. Hence, I stood before the seated clerk whose khakis stretched over a teasing crotch and spread legs. Bobby looked like he had graduated from high school the day before and even had a zit or two on his chin to prove it. Tall, slim and "cute" was our company clerk. The wagon was filling up like a New York subway car at rush hour, all passengers toting a rifle. I was pushed over Bobby until my crotch was flush with his dewy lips. He tugged on my belt and pulled me down until I was seated on his lap. "Better on my knee than in my mouth," he said.

"Thanks," I answered, pressing my hip into a package I would love to open Christmas morning.

The cab lurched forward and its cargo heaved backward. Bobby clung to my belt, his thumb rubbing the elastic band of my shorts. Was he telling me something? I tested the water by giving his basket a few more hip rubs. He squeezed my waist, a finger now inside the band of my jockeys. Was this really happening? I was surrounded by fifty guys, all armed, in a fucking convoy.

Bobby's fingers pulled up my khaki shirt so that he could get them inside my shorts, inches above my ass. My cock grew to its full height: seven inches, give or take a few centimeters. My hip told me Bobby's prick was also standing at attention.

I lost my head and tugged at his fly zipper. He kept his and stopped me.

"After chow, in my office."

I squeezed his dick. He caressed my undershorts. Love, army style.

I asked Sergeant Baker for permission to speak to the company clerk on personal business. (Ha-ha.) I said I would rather do this on my own time than take time off from my training. Sergeant Baker liked that. A little brown nosing never hurt and how I would love to brown nose Sergeant Baker's back door.

Headquarters was a glorified shack across from the barracks that housed the noncoms, including my Sergeant Baker. Bobby bunked in a room behind the office, using the barracks facilities to shit, shower and shave. Nice digs, and all because he was computer literate. The captain and staff sergeant were long gone. Bobby was waiting for me dressed in fatigues that bloused over his boots, like a combat hero between wars. His shirt was open to reveal his dog tags hanging atop a hairless chest. He was rubbing his dick and showed me the rigid bulge that ran down his inner thigh. I rubbed my crotch to let him know I was just as horny and eager to suck or fuck or anything else he may have had in mind.

He looked like forbidden fruit (i.e., underage) so I took him in my arms and began by kissing him full on those tender lips. Our tongues entwined as we indulged in a Princeton Rub, cock to cock. Inserting his hand between us, Bobby began to feel my cock. I immediately extended him the same courtesy.

I stuck my tongue deep down his throat. He tasted of chewing tobacco and smelled of cheap aftershave, both of which made my hard cock begin to seep cum cream.

"Be nice to me and you'll never pull KP or any shit detail again."

"What do I have to do to be nice?" I asked, hoping for the best.

"Suck my prick."

I went to my knees, feeling I was getting the better part of the deal. The zipper that had eluded me that afternoon now yielded to my touch. I reached in, inhaling the erotic aroma of ball sweat, and took out his prick. I refrained from whistling at the sight and settled for licking my lips. I wasn't going to get my first taste of foreskin, but I was going to lavish my mouth over a redheaded lady-pleaser with a slight upward curve and leaking a fine sliver of Bobby-boy's cum juice. I cleared the clogged piss-hole with my tongue, causing Bobby to order me: "Eat my joy juice. Eat my fucking joy juice."

Joy juice? Before my Army days came to an end I would compose a lexicon of poetic names for semen. I sucked, my lips caressing the rigid flesh, grazing over the big red head and the telltale ring of his circumcision. He began to fuck my face, which I encouraged by wrapping my arms around his ass, kneading the flesh and looking to gain entrance to the crack and find his tender hole.

My stud was hopping on one foot and salivating. Fearing he would release his joy juice too soon I eased his prick out of my mouth, held it in my hand, inspected it at close range, rubbed the head under my nose, masturbated the firm shaft and tongued the tiny opening.

Reaching into the fly, I pulled out his balls. A generous handful. "Take 'em in your mouth," Bobby ordered.

Opening wide, I got one nut in and sucked on it. With his fingers, Bobby eased the twin nuts between my lips. I lapped the mouthful of scrotum while Bobby rubbed his cock between his belly and my forehead. "Warm up the cream," he laughed. "You like it nice and hot, right?" I gave his balls a reassuring suck to let him know that was how I liked it.

I savored the man sac for as long as I could take it but the need to breathe forced me to give up my prize. The void was quickly filled by Bobby's cock, which he guided between my lips. "I'm near," he panted, fucking my face with long strokes, withdrawing completely before shoving it back down my throat. I began to taste the first drops of his joy juice. His release was so close I could feel his ass muscles tense under my probing hands. I got a finger into his asscrack and poked his hole. He raised one of his legs and wrapped it around my neck. I got a good inch up his ass. He shoved the entire length of his cock into my mouth so that my nose was buried in his fly, sniffing his bush.

He yelled, "Fuck!" and ejaculated into my mouth. One, two, three, four squirts of thick, warm jism. He fired it like a machine gun, so quick I swallowed the streams without tasting them. I opened my fly, pulled out my dick and began rubbing. I looked up at Bobby who was cleaning his cock with a handkerchief, his balls hanging over my face. In less than a minute I shot a load as big as the company clerk's, completing our personal business.

He rubbed his cock across my lips. "Kiss it good night."

I did.

I never pulled KP or a shit detail for the remainder of my training. It's who you blow that counts in this man's army.

The final week of basic training would be a bivouac. Camping out and living as if in combat. The base was alive with rumors and talk of pup tents measuring six by four. Two men to a tent. Well, that gave one pause. Who would I bunk with? Could I choose a buddy? I asked our company clerk if I could pick my tent mate. No fucking way. "We make up the list and post it the night before you leave on bivouac."

"Give me Julio Zapata."

"So you got a hard-on for the Cuban jalapeño? You could burn your tongue nibbling on that. Maybe I will and maybe I won't."

I got off detail by blowing the clerk so... "I'll kiss your ass, Bobby."

No yes or no this time. "My place tonight," was his answer.

I pretended to go to the latrine and detoured to HQ. Bobby was waiting for me in his room with a bare ass and a stiff dick. This kid was a WASP jalapeño. "Bend over and take my picture, Bobby-boy." He bent, spread his checks and showed me his camera. The lens was hairless, tan and puckered for the shot. I was once again on my knees for the company clerk, this time in a trade-off, or so I hoped.

Our clerk wiggled his hot ass and intoned. "*Click. Click. Click,* ass licker, go for it."

I sniffed up the crack—not bad—then got the tip of my tongue on the poop hole. Bobby jerked up as I made contact. I licked the tender lips, first dutifully, then passionately. This A-hole was so good it had me tonguing up and down then in and out. "Deeper," he yelled, shoving his ass in my face. Holding his hips for a firm grip I got my tongue in about two inches. The flesh there was so tender, so yielding. I guessed Bobby was a virgin. I was teasing his cherry with my tongue. The thought had me creaming in my pants.

"Fuck my ass," he cried, and his fist brought on his orgasm, spending in jet streams of cum cream.

My jism was dripping like piss. I unzipped, fisted and dropped a load to equal his.

"Kiss my ass good night," he ordered.

I did.

The list was posted the Sunday night before the Monday morning bivouac. Two hundred guys elbowed their way to the board. I saw Julio up front—saw him read it and turn back. He spotted me in the crowd and made his way to me. "Looks like you and me are asshole buddies, pal."

I almost fainted.

Was I the first soldier in history to have a hard-on while setting up a six-by-four pup tent? Julio was a tall jalapeño. He would have to sleep with his legs bent or wrapped around my neck. Should I give him the choice? I didn't have much time to think about it, as it was a grueling day of marching, crawling and eating out of a mess kit. *Mess* is the operative word. The sun set, the clouds rolled in and the rain began to fall. Just what we needed.

Exhausted, we retired to our tent, hoping it didn't leak. Julio stripped down to his boxers and stretched out, his toes touching the tent's flap. I got down to my jockeys and lay down beside him. Our arms and legs were inches apart. When my eyes adjusted to the dark I could see Julio tracing the line of hair that ran down his chest to the elastic band of his shorts. His fingers inched under the band. Was he going to...? I could see the outline of his cock inside his boxers. Was it hard or was the dark playing a trick on me? He took a deep breath and started to snore.

Well, no one promised me a honeymoon on my first bivouac.

I wanted to lick his skivvies. Tease his cock out of his fly then skin back his beautiful foreskin with my lips. I wanted to jack off. Alas, I could do none of the above.

I dozed an hour then awoke on this rainy night. I glanced at my tent mate and thought I was dreaming. Julio's cock was sticking straight out of his fly, listing slightly to his belly button. It was big, thick and sporting a drop of morning dew on its tip. His erection had peeled the foreskin so that it covered half the cock's head. I wiggled around the tent pole without bringing it down on our heads. My nose was so close to Julio's prick I could smell it. I was at the point of no return. Kill me he might, but I was going to do it. Yes. I was going to do what I had dreamed of doing since I first laid eyes on Julio Zapata.

I put my lips over the head of his cock, drinking in the aroma. I caressed the foreskin and slowly pulled it down to uncover the cockhead. As delicious as I had imagined it? No. More so. Much, much more so. My sleeping beauty sighed in his sleep. I began to suck, slowly, engaging my tongue to ride the foreskin up and down the shaft, covering and uncovering the big head. If I got caught I would die with my boots off and Julio Zapata's cock in my mouth.

"What the fuck are you doing?" My hero was awake.

"Blowing you. You want me to stop?"

"Are you a fucking queer?"

"I'm queer for you, Julio."

"You're the only guy who ever said my name right."

"That's because I love you, Julio."

"You gonna swallow my cum juice?"

"Every fucking drop."

"Go for it, cocksucker."

And I did.

"Don't pull the skin all the way up. I'll pop too quick. Suck the shaft and keep off the head." For this being his first gay blow job, he certainly knew what he wanted.

I followed his instructions, eager to please and learn the dos and don'ts of sucking uncut cock. Julio inhaled and spread his long legs wide open as if inviting me in. Easing his cock out of my mouth I began to explore the terrain. I stuck my nose in his curly bush, sniffing; ran my tongue up his belly and into his belly button. He giggled. Moving up, I kissed his hairy chest, his pointed, pink tits, his neck. I looked into his smiling face. His dark eyes were fixed on me. He was licking his lips. "Suck me more." My lips touched his. He hesitated a moment, then grabbed the back of my neck and stuck his tongue in my mouth. Cum cream shot out of my dick. He shoved my head down to where he wanted it, and I was at the mercy of my Cuban lover whose huge cock dripped semen into the puckered rim of his foreskin bunched up below the head.

"Lick me clean," he instructed. I pulled off my shorts and went to it, savoring every drop, sticking my tongue under the foreskin and lapping the juice of love only Julio could feed me. My cock leaked cum like it was piss.

Julio wrapped his legs around my neck for the supreme moment when his cock gushed squirt after squirt of warm jism down my throat. He held my head on his cock until the well ran dry. We didn't move for a good five minutes, exulting in the afterglow of our rapture.

"You're a good cocksucker," my hero complimented me.

"We'll be in this tent for another four days," I reminded him.

"I got a good supply of raincoats," Julio told me.

"You took raincoats on bivouac. Why?"

"Because I heard it might rain."

I kissed his balls. He lay back, stretched as best he could in our six-by-four home and began snoring. I got up and went out to take a piss.

I was nude but it was midnight, at least, and the rain had stopped. The sky was clearing and now riddled with stars. A half moon appeared and cast an eerie glow over the sleeping camp. I needed a cold drink but hated to rid my mouth of the taste of Julio's generous secretions. I was elated, giddy and perhaps in love. I was also hearing voices coming from the area of our outhouse. I moved in closer. The sounds were coming from behind the outhouse. I approached and peered around the corner.

There were three people there, one of them kneeling. What the fuck was this? Unless I was hallucinating it was the staff sergeant, John Caputo, bending over our company clerk, fucking the shit out of him; literally and figuratively speaking, I'm sure. Standing over the buggering couple was our Sergeant Billy Baker, his prick sticking out of his boxers as he egged on his buddy, Caputo.

I doubt Bobby was being raped as he was bucking his ass into Sergeant Caputo, bouncing up and down as Caputo's long, fat prick worked the clerk's back passage.

"You want sloppy seconds?" Caputo offered Sergeant Baker.

"I'll fuck his mouth first," Sergeant Baker said, grabbing Bobby's head and shoving his cock in the clerk's open mouth.

I thought it was time for me to make my presence known. "Can I be of assistance?" I volunteered.

"What the fuck are you doing here?" Sergeant Baker snapped at me, his prick deep down Bobby's throat.

"I came to take a piss. What are you doing?"

"What does it look like we're doing, Private? We're taking the company clerk's cherry. It's a bivouac tradition," was Baker's explanation of the midnight fuck.

Bobby was getting it front and rear from two of the finest pricks on the base and he owed it all to being a computer wiz. Will wonders never cease?

My eyes were on Baker's cock, fucking Bobby's mouth. I'd wanted a look at that since day one of our basic training. I bent closer and sniffed Sergeant Baker's balls. He freed his cock from Bobby's eager lips and, as I had suspected, it was generous in length and girth and sported a foreskin that completely covered the head, ending in a tight hump around the pee-pee hole. I skinned him back and kissed the head.

"You've got enough hangover to dock me," I told him.

"Yeah, dock him," Caputo urged, not missing a stroke.

"That's queer," Baker said.

"Dock him, then fuck him, if it makes you feel better," the ever-inventive Caputo advised.

Sergeant Baker liked that and so did I. He bent to get his dick in line with mine.

My cock was still flaccid after my explosion with Julio and just perfect for what Sergeant Baker intended. When our dicks kissed he pulled up the foreskin to encase it over my cock's head.

I was docked with Sergeant Baker. It was more thrilling than anything I had ever done. It was warm, it was intoxicating, it was FANFUCKINGTASTIC. If this was bivouac, *vive la guerre*.

"I'm going to cream," Caputo shouted.

"Me too," young Bobby cried, bucking his ass into Caputo's ejaculating dick.

I had my fist wrapped around my cock, rubbing the head with the sergeant's prepuce. Caputo and Bobby were in their rapture. I took a chance and kissed Sergeant Baker on his lips. He responded by sticking his tongue in my mouth.

I could no longer put off what I had come here to do. "I have to piss," I told my sergeant.

He put his lips to my ear and whispered. "Go for it."

* * *

Bivouac is the hands-on phase of basic training that turns raw recruits into soldiers. Don't think, even for a moment, that the new Army, with its acceptance of gays, is less rigorous in simulating wartime conditions when leaving the civilized comforts of camp for life in the raw. In fact, Julio and I were convinced it was more spartan than ever; an apt description as Sparta, remember, was home to the army of lovers who reigned supreme in ancient Greece.

We returned to our tent each night, exhausted but pleased that we had not only survived but grown in body and spirit. We ate our rations (ugh), showered in cold water (shiver) and fell into each other's arms for warmth and comfort. Like millions of fighting men before our time, we became comrades in arms. I told Julio about the cruising area behind the outhouse. We took a peek that night and caught sergeants Baker and Caputo enjoying a circle jerk with a black recruit.

"You want to join in?" I asked Julio.

"Let's go home," he answered with his hand on my bare ass.

HOME?

Yeah, that pup tent was our home and Julio, with his body pressed against me, made it clear that we comrades were now lovers.

MARINE GUARD

Dirk Strong

When I arrived in Rome in March, the city was jammed with tourists preparing for Easter week. The Triduum, or three-day period just before Easter Sunday, was a whirlwind of activity, and the congestion made it incredibly difficult to navigate the couple of blocks from my apartment to my new job as a consular officer at the U.S. Embassy.

I finally made it to the Palazzo Margherita, a grand century-old Renaissance-style palace on the Via Vittorio Veneto. Once the residence of Queen Margherita of Savoy, the widow of King Umberto I of Italy, it was acquired by the American government in 1946. Palm trees stood sentinel outside the iron fence, and entrance to the building itself was controlled by an arched gateway staffed by members of the Marine Security Guard.

I stepped up to the gate juggling a briefcase, a laptop and a Rollaboard suitcase filled with a couple of changes of clothes to keep in my office. In the diplomatic corps you have to be prepared for almost anything. The Marine guard on duty was six-foot-two of gorgeous manflesh—jarhead haircut over a model-handsome face with sharply etched features, broad shoulders shoehorned into a dress uniform, narrow waist, perfectly creased blue slacks and spit-shined black dress shoes.

I dropped my briefcase on his foot as I fumbled in my pocket for my ID. "My name is Adam Burr," I said, finally retrieving my ID. "I'm starting today."

The Marine, whose badge said his name was Roemer, looked me up and down, and I felt a shiver of sexual anticipation run through my body. He reviewed my credentials. "As long as you're not Aaron Burr," he said, handing them back to me. "Remember, no illegal dueling on embassy property."

"I'll keep my eye out for Hamiltons," I said, and that's when Lucas Roemer and I shared our first smile. Late that night, back in my apartment, I remembered that smile and used it to fuel my first jack-off in my new position.

My job was to help U.S. citizens abroad who lost their passports, got into trouble with the law or otherwise needed assistance navigating the intricate Roman bureaucracy. I loved my job, because in addition to the requisite desk work, I got to travel around the city meeting with officials and solving problems.

The best part of the job was returning to the embassy when Lucas Roemer was on guard duty. The primary mission of the Marine Security Guard was to provide internal security for government secrets and information. The secondary mission of his detachment was to provide protection for U.S. citizens and U.S government property located within the embassy. I wanted to acquire Lucas's protective services personally—but the military's pesky Don't Ask, Don't Tell meant that any connection between Lucas and me would have to remain an erotic fantasy rather than a reality.

From that first shared smile, I had a feeling that Lucas was gay. The next time that he and I talked, we were in the gardens behind the embassy in early May. I had just finished escorting a delegation from a tractor manufacturer interested in selling to Italy, and I took a moment to relax beside the fountain featuring a marble statue of the god Triton blowing a conch shell spouting water. Lucas caught me checking out the god's endowment, which looked pretty good since I hadn't seen another man's dick in person in too long.

"Seems like the water's coming out the wrong place," Lucas said, with a sly smile, as he passed me.

"This isn't Brussels," I said, referring to the Manneken Pis, the famous fountain featuring a pissing cherub.

"I've seen it," Lucas said. "Triton there has him beat."

I looked at Lucas. His light blue eyes were sparkling. Was he flirting with me? The Don't Ask, Don't Tell legislation pushed through under the Clinton administration was under fire in Washington then, and it looked like it was going to be repealed. Could Lucas Roemer be gay? Was there a chance I'd find out for myself, if the legislation disappeared?

"Yeah, but have you seen Michelangelo's *David?*" I asked. "There's a guy with a big weapon."

Lucas guffawed, and shook his head. "See you around, Adam Burr."

I shivered with pleasure at the thought that he'd remembered my name. He probably knew everyone who worked in the embassy by name and sight; that was part of his job. But I was willing to hope that he'd taken a special interest in me.

I thought about Lucas more than I should have. But he was just so damn handsome. One day I looked out the window of my office and saw him and a bunch of his fellow Marines posing for a photo op with some of the Italian *carabinieri*. The Italians wore capes and tricorn hats with red plumes. Next to the butch

Marines in their brass-studded jackets and formfitting red-striped pants, they looked like they couldn't fight their way out of paper bags. Lucas, of course, was the butchest of the lot.

I drifted off into an erotic fantasy of him right there at my desk, when I was supposed to be sorting out a passport problem for a student from Illinois. I was undoing those brass buttons of his, one by one, then unbuckling the white belt around his waist to find that he wasn't wearing a shirt underneath his jacket.

"Aaron?"

I looked up to see my boss standing in the doorway to my office, and I was very glad that my desk camouflaged my hard-on. "Got a minute to handle a problem for me?"

"Certainly, sir," I said, grabbing my appointment book to cover my groin as I stood.

The embassy sponsored a party in the gardens to celebrate Labor Day, and though Lucas was on duty, I managed to find myself near him for a few minutes and strike up a conversation. I said something innocuous about the embassy building and then mentioned, "They say a queen used to live here."

He leaned conspiratorially toward me. "I see queens going in and out of here every day."

"Present company excepted," I said. "Nobody's ever called me a queen."

"You might look good in drag, though," he said.

I blushed and turned away, then got caught up in a conversation with one of the political officers. I didn't see Lucas again for a couple of days, but that wasn't unusual; the Marines had varying schedules on the embassy gates.

I was surprised by the knock on my door. I had no friends in Rome other than my coworkers, and I doubted any of them would seek out my apartment so soon after the end of the workday. I'd only been home for a few minutes—just enough time to pull off my suit jacket and undo my tie, and kick my black dress shoes off.

I looked through the peephole and was astonished to see Lucas Roemer. I undid the chain and pulled the door open. He was wearing jeans and a long-sleeved polo shirt, and carrying a bottle of champagne. "I was hoping you'd celebrate with me," he said.

"Celebrate what?"

"Don't Ask, Don't Tell is history," he said.

"Sounds like a reason to celebrate." I stepped back to let him in, but instead of walking past me he leaned forward and kissed me. His lips were feathery light against mine at first then pressed forward with an urgency that took me by surprise but was quickly reciprocated.

"I've been waiting a long time to do that," he said, when he finally pulled back.

I took a deep breath. "Wow. That was even better than I imagined it might be."

He smiled slyly. "Well, then let me prepare to blow your mind."

He stepped inside, and I closed the door behind him. He positioned the bottle of sparkling wine between his legs and peeled off the tinny covering. I wanted to get glasses out of the cabinet—but I was entranced by the sight of that large thickness sprouting from between Lucas's legs.

"Can I help with that?" I asked.

He looked at me and smiled. "If you'd like."

I knelt down and wrapped my left hand around the hardness, and his hand covered mine. I used my right hand to untwist the cage over the cork. "Better back away," he said. "Might be dangerous when this thing shoots."

I stood up. "Can you hold back for a second?"

"It's going to be tough."

"You're a Marine. Butch it up."

I walked over to the kitchen and grabbed two tall, slim glasses, the closest thing I had to champagne flutes. I returned to the living room, and with a quick twist of his strong right hand, Lucas extracted the cork and golden fluid bubbled out. I caught it in the first glass, and then he poured the second and set the bottle on my coffee table.

I handed him one glass and lifted the other. "To a celebration," I said.

He clinked his glass against mine then twined his arm around mine before he lifted the glass to his lips. My heart jumped. A handsome Marine who was both sexy and sweet? Talk about a walking wet dream.

We looked into each other's eyes as we sipped our champagne. When we extracted ourselves, he kissed me again, his lips tasting like the sparkling wine.

"What do you say we take this into your bedroom?" he asked.

"I say follow me." I grabbed my champagne glass and the bottle, and led the way to my bedroom, glad I had remembered to make the bed that morning, though I was sure it would get unmade very quickly.

In one quick move, Lucas pulled his polo shirt over his head, revealing a squarish chest with large brown nipples, and a treasure trail of black hair that ran from between his pecs down to his belly button, an outie. He had washboard abs and a narrow waist.

I leaned forward and took his right nipple gently between my teeth. He groaned and tilted his head back. As I slurped and nibbled, he busied his fingers unbuttoning my dress shirt then slipping it back over my shoulders. I switched nipples, and he ran his hands over my shoulders, pinching and kneading the tense muscles there.

I pulled back and we kissed again, our chests pressed together. Mine was much hairier than his, and Lucas seemed to like sliding against me. He pulled his lips away and arched his back again, almost like a cat, rubbing his chest against mine.

His fingers fumbled with my belt buckle, and I helped him along. Once undone, my pants slipped off my hips and pooled at the floor and I stepped out of them, wearing only my boxers and my socks. I knelt to the ground in front of Lucas and pressed my face against his groin, feeling the warmth of his stiff dick through his jeans. I rubbed my cheek against it and he moaned, pressing my head to him.

He unbuckled his belt and undid his jeans. They were molded to his body, unlike my dress pants, and I had to peel them back, revealing a pair of simple white jockey shorts. His stiffy was outlined against the fabric, a circle of precum already staining the fabric.

I stood up and turned my back to him, and he did just what I wanted—he pulled me to him, so that my ass was pressed back against his groin. His hands reached around my chest to my nipples, and he leaned down to kiss my neck. I reached back to his hips, sticking my fingers under the waistband of his jockeys.

We swayed like that for a moment or two, until he nibbled on my ear and whispered "If we keep doing this I'm going to shoot off in my shorts."

"Wouldn't want to waste anything," I said, stepping out of his grasp and turning around. "We are under austerity measures, you know."

I went down on my knees again, this time peeling back his jockeys to reveal his dick, long and slim and curved like a banana. I licked my tongue up the length and he rocked on his feet, grabbing my bureau for support.

I appreciated the plush carpeting in my bedroom as I knelt before Lucas Roemer, tonguing his balls, tickling his piss-slit with my tongue and inhaling the scent that rose from his pubic hair. I began to swallow his dick an inch at a time, going down and pulling back, gradually relaxing my throat muscles enough to take him completely inside me.

"Oh, man," he moaned, the first time I buried my nose in his bush, his dick fully inside my throat. I began suctioning him, lightly at first, then with intent, and his body quivered and he began making some very un-Marine-like whimpers.

I knew I ought to back off, make this pleasure last—but I couldn't help myself. I was a greedy bastard, and I wanted to swallow Lucas's cum—and I wanted it now. I grabbed his asscheeks and began jamming my head up and down on his cock, and his body shook and he erupted down my throat with a howl that seemed part pain and part sheer ecstasy.

He took a deep breath and slid back against the bureau. "I want to slap every member of Congress upside the head right about now," he said.

"Why?"

"For making me wait this long to be here with you. If they'd never created such a dumb-ass law we could have been fucking since you landed in Rome."

"You never know," I said. "You could have found somebody else before I even got here."

He shook his head. "I was waiting for you. I just didn't know it until you showed up."

He stood up and reached over to my boxers. My dick had already popped through the opening, and he grabbed it in his right hand, which felt warm and strong around me.

"Oh yeah," I said.

He leaned forward and kissed me again, as he wrapped his hand around my dick and began stroking me, lubricated only by my precum. My senses were overwhelmed—the taste of Lucas in my mouth, his smell in my nostrils, the roughness of his hand against my tender dick.

I came too quickly, shooting off in his hand and dribbling onto my boxers. Lucas released my dick and smeared my own cum down my chest—then pressed his chest against mine so my fluids mingled onto his smooth chest.

I kicked off my socks and dropped my boxers, and we fell down onto my bed together, wrestling naked on the spread. I'd never been much of an athlete, but they made us wrestle in high school and I still remembered a couple of holds. I wasn't sure if I really overpowered Lucas or he just let me win because he wanted me on top of him.

"So, who's the big, tough Marine now?" I asked, straddling him, holding his biceps down on the bed.

In a minute, he had me flipped and lying on my chest with him on top of me. "That would be me," he said, laughing.

He began to give me a back rub, kneading my tense shoulders once again. "You really need to relax, Adam," he said. "I know a great place with masseurs who know their stuff. You'll have to go there with me sometime."

"They do couples massage there?" I asked, my head flat against my pillow.

"We'll see what we can work out. You have any oil I can use?"

"There's some body lotion in the bathroom cabinet."

"Be right back."

The bed sprang up a bit when he hopped off, and immediately I missed the pressure and warmth of his body against mine. Fortunately he was back a moment later. "Nice selection of product," he said. "We share the same taste in lube."

"I didn't realize Marines had taste," I said.

"Ooh, somebody's getting cheeky," he said, slapping my butt. "Tell me, does spanking give you a hard-on?"

"Everything about you gives me a hard-on," I mumbled into the pillow.

"Good answer."

He squirted some body lotion in his hands and began rubbing down my back with long, smooth strokes. He slapped my buttcheeks a few times and then began to stroke my perineum. "Every guy has his own G-spot," he said. "The trick is to find it. I always like to know what I'm dealing with."

I shivered and moaned at the touch of his fingertip stroking the tender area between my ass and balls. He squirted some lube on his finger and began penetrating me, a millimeter at a time. His fingertip was slightly rough against my tight channel. "Did you know that in your twenties, your prostate is only the size of a walnut?" he asked, as he inched his finger deeper into me. "It gets bigger over time."

"Other body parts do that, too," I said.

"Mmm-hmm," he said.

His finger must have been in to the second knuckle when I felt it reach my prostate. I bucked beneath him and he said, "So, that's yours. Good to know."

He pulled his finger back and widened my ass, and then stuck two fingers inside, snaking their way up my channel until the longer of the two reached my prostate again. In slow, lazy strokes he began pressing against it, sending waves of pleasure through me.

I was zoning out to the pleasure when I heard the unmistakable sound of a condom package ripping, and then more squirts of lube. Lucas pried open my ass once again and the head of his dick nosed against the opening.

"Oh, yeah, look at that little rose, just winking at me," he said. "Papa's got a special present for you."

He slid right into me, and then lowered himself so that his body was resting on mine. The weight was intense, pressing me into the bed, and I was having trouble breathing, but it felt so good to be enveloped by him as he kissed my neck.

Then he levered himself up on his elbows and began to fuck me. Long, slow strokes at first, the way he'd been stimulating my prostate. Then the passion overtook him and he began slamming into me.

He pulled back. "I want to see your face. Turn over."

My ass was cold and wet and empty. I flipped over onto my back and looked up at Lucas's handsome face. A droplet of sweat dripped down from his forehead, and his blue eyes were dark and glazed with lust. He pulled my legs up and rested them on his shoulders, and then positioned his dick for another assault.

If being fucked into the pillow by Lucas was awesome, it was a whole other level of amazing to look into his eyes as he drove his dick into my ass. With one hand he reached down and grabbed my dick and began to jerk me in time with his thrusts.

This time we were both making those very un-Marine-like whimpers, both of us gasping and whimpering and staring as our dicks erupted almost simultaneously. Lucas pulled out of me, let my legs down and then sprawled on the bed beside me.

I wanted another glass of champagne, but I was feeling too lazy to get up and get one, and looking at Lucas I could tell he felt the same way. I closed my eyes, just for a moment—and when I opened them again nearly two hours had passed, my stomach was grumbling and I had to pee.

I crawled out of bed, careful not to wake Lucas, and stumbled to the bathroom. I stood over the toilet and aimed my stream, and a moment later Lucas was beside me, doing the same thing. It was such an intimate moment, pissing together—but just one more bit of intimacy after all that had happened so far that evening.

"I'd kill for a burger," Lucas said, after he shook the last drops of urine from his dick.

I did the same, and flushed. "I can't offer you a burger, but I make a mean plate of pasta," I said.

"Bring it on."

I grabbed a bathrobe and went out to the kitchen. "I'm going to take a quick shower," he called as I began preparing the food.

My grandmother on my mother's side was Italian, and from her I learned the secret to making Sunday gravy—a slow-simmered tomato sauce with mushrooms, garlic and bite-sized meatballs. Once a month or so I spent a weekend afternoon making up a batch and then freezing it in containers.

I began boiling the water for some handmade spiral pasta that I bought at the local market, and set a frozen lump of sauce on low heat. By the time I had everything going, Lucas appeared wrapped in a big white towel. "Smells good," he said.

"Keep an eye on everything while I clean up," I said.

I hurried through a shower, slipped my bathrobe back on, and by the time I got back to the kitchen the pasta was al dente and the sauce warmed through. Lucas sat at the table and I drained the pasta then ladled it out to two flat bowls, covered with sauce and meatballs. Then I grated some fresh Parmesan cheese and brought the plates to the table.

"This night is getting better and better," Lucas said.

We ate the pasta, making the kind of small talk you do on

what was essentially a first date—where we'd grown up, gone to school and so on.

Lucas finished the last bit of pasta in his bowl, wiped his lips, and said, "Amazing sex, delicious meal. I guess I should get out now before something goes wrong."

"What about dessert?" I pouted.

"You have something?"

I stood up before him and slipped my robe off. My dick sprang forward. "How's this?"

"Looks like more than a mouthful," he said. He licked his lips and leaned down to take me in his mouth.

The angle was awkward, though, so we went back to the bedroom. This time I pulled back the covers and lay down on my cool white sheets, resting my head on the pillows. Lucas lost the towel and climbed up on the bed, kneeling before me and taking my dick in his mouth. He sucked for a minute or two until I said, "Turn around."

He lay down next to me, his head by my dick and my head at his dick, and we began sucking each other. It took us both a while to come—it was the third time that night after all—and we got to practice all the techniques we knew on each other. He came first, and I swallowed what he had and then he kept sucking me until I came. Then he squirmed around so we were facing each other once again.

"So, was it worth the wait?" I asked lazily, looking at him.

"Don't ask, and I won't tell," he said.

I elbowed him.

"Baby, you have no idea," he said. "But I'm telling you one thing. You are mine and I am yours and nothing, no act of Congress or presidential decree, is going to change that."

SO, THEN

Emily Moreton

S o." Mike waited for Danny to settle back in the bed, then curled into him, thigh against Danny's damaged leg, where the warmth would soak into him. Danny made a small, contented noise and pulled the dark green covers tighter over their shoulders. One arm stayed around Mike, holding him in place.

In Mike's opinion, post-sex cuddling was one of the best things about being on land. Navy bunks really weren't made for two people, and anyway, it was one thing to fuck around with a shipmate. Flaunting it in front of a ship full of people who'd left their own partners behind always felt sort of cruel.

"So what?" Danny asked.

Mike pushed aside his sleepy fuzziness, his drifting thoughts about his shipmates and the warm closeness of his oldest friend, now sort-of boyfriend, trying to remember what he'd intended to say.

"You know we're only shipping out for three weeks this time?"

Danny stiffened slightly under him, probably at the reminder that this was their last night together. Considering they hadn't seen each other in two years, a week had been more than enough time to feel like this was how things always were. Which didn't make a lot of sense, even in Mike's head, but was true nevertheless. Leaving Danny this time was going to be easily as unpleasant as leaving him right after college to go into the Navy.

"Yeah," Danny said softly.

Mike swallowed the urge to say something about leaving. It would either come out maudlin or overly cheerful, and he wasn't sure which was worse. Also, it really was only three weeks, and he was determined not to let himself get stupid over it. "So, we'll be back a couple of days before Pride. And I thought maybe we could go watch the parade. Hit a couple of bars after."

Danny tensed even more; so much so that Mike was half-grateful for the excuse when Danny nudged him away and sat up. Danny was frowning, which looked really weird under his sex-mussed blond hair. Not that Mike's position, looking up at Danny from on his back, really helped.

"You really think no one else from your ship will be there?" Danny's voice clearly implied that Mike was a naïve fool, which was not exactly Mike's favorite iteration of Danny's personality.

"Nooo." Mike drew the word out in lieu of rolling his eyes. "I think it's been okay for me to be gay in the Navy for a good couple of years, and that anyone from my ship who is there won't care."

Danny didn't stop frowning, but his blue eyes were more worried than annoyed, and it melted most of Mike's faint irritation. Mike rolled over, resting his chin on Danny's hip. He could just about see Danny's face from that position, though it felt like he was straining his eyeballs looking up. "It's fine," he said firmly. "I've got good friends out there, I'm safe. I mean, I'm not planning on hitting on my CO anytime soon, but that's mostly because he's married and old enough to be my dad."

"He kind of makes it work," Danny said thoughtfully. Mike couldn't really argue with that—the colonel pretty much epitomized silver fox in a way that had featured in more than one of Mike's fantasies.

"You hit on him, then."

Danny laughed softly, his stomach twitching with it, and Mike smiled into Danny's skin. "You don't have to worry about me, you know," he said.

"You're in the Navy; it's not exactly the safest profession ever." Danny petted Mike's hair, which never failed to make Mike feel like purring.

"You don't have to worry about me being gay in the Navy," he amended. "I want you to meet some of the guys. They want to meet you, too."

"You talk about me to them?" Danny asked, more surprised than Mike would have expected.

Mike tipped his head up, dislodging Danny's hand down to the back of his neck. "Of course. Tell them how brilliant you are, tell them how gorgeous you are, tell them they should all be jealous of how good you are in bed..."

Danny flushed bright red, which was adorable and weird and made Mike want to kiss him. Danny really was brilliant and gorgeous and amazing in bed, and Mike could kiss him if he wanted to. He pushed himself up to his knees and leaned in, cupping the back of Danny's neck.

"You trying to distract me?" Danny asked, mouth quirking up in a smile.

Mike stroked Danny's good thigh, not quite soft enough to tickle as he rubbed the hairs the wrong way. "Is it working?"

Danny's breath caught when Mike brushed fingers over his half-hard cock. "Not so far."

"Ouch! I'm naked and feeling you up and you're, what, thinking about your dry cleaning?" Mike curled his hand loosely over Danny.

"I'm an academic, I can't afford dry cleaning. But, now that you mention it, you do need to pick up your uniform." Danny stared hard at Mike, obviously trying to look unaffected. It didn't quite work, given how his face flushed slightly when Mike cupped his palm over the head of Danny's cock. "I don't want you to forget and have to head out naked."

Mike ducked his head, laughing against Danny's neck. Being back with Danny was great; there were years of history between them that he couldn't replicate with his closest friends on his ship. "I missed you."

"I—" Mike felt Danny draw in a deep breath, but he didn't say anything, just kissed Mike's ear, then down his jaw. Mike lifted his head to meet Danny's mouth on his, one hand moving to Danny's shoulder for balance. Danny slipped his tongue into Mike's mouth, and Mike tightened his hold on Danny.

"Fuck," Danny said against his mouth. Right, Mike still had one hand on Danny's dick, now hot and hard in his hand. "You gonna do something there, or what?"

Mike loosened his grip so he could straddle Danny's thigh, then stroked slowly up the length of him. Danny made a small, pleased sound and kissed Mike again, a hand returning to the back of his neck to hold him close. Mike kissed him back, palming the head of his cock on every stroke. He couldn't stop himself grinning at the little noises Danny made, the way his hips twitched slightly, pushing him into Mike's hand.

Danny wasn't going to last, Mike knew—he couldn't always get it up for a second time in one night, but when he did, he never lasted. Mike leaned in, pushing Danny back into the headboard, looming over him just a little, just enough to make Danny's breath catch again as he came.

Mike eased him through it, kissing the corner of his mouth and the edge of his cheek until Danny fumbled to knock his hand away.

"You were saying?" Mike asked.

Danny rolled his head against the wall till he and Mike made eye contact. Danny's hair was a mess, his eyes heavy and his face flushed. "Fuck if I know."

Mike grinned, rocking a little against Danny's thigh, caught between wanting that, and wanting to jerk himself off, his hand wet with Danny's come. Danny caught his hips, pulling him in till his dick was tight against Danny, and okay, maybe Mike did know what he wanted after all.

"Just like that," Danny said, low in his ear. "That's it, just like that, you're so hot."

Speaking of not really lasting long the second time around— it took Mike less than three minutes to come all over Danny's skin. Best three minutes he'd had since the last time, though.

And he wanted to, so he did, putting an end to any kind of conversation not including the words *yes, more,* or *right there, fuck, don't stop.*

"So," Freddie said, when Mike got back to the tiny cabin they shared with two other guys. Freddie's stuff, to Mike's complete lack of surprise, was already put neatly away, and Freddie himself was back in uniform, sprawled on the top bunk, one leg dangling in Mike's face. The guy really was too tall to be in the Navy, which was all about tiny spaces. "He's the guy."

Mike automatically checked for James and Luke, even though their stuff was conspicuously missing. Not that either man would care if they walked in on Mike and Freddie talking about guys, but they kept the chat about women to a minimum, and Mike always felt he owed them the same courtesy.

"Yeah, he's—hang on, you're here, how did you even see us?"

Freddie raised one eyebrow, which he said made him look mysterious and Mike made him look like a loon. "I see everything."

"Not through three decks and more walls than I can be bothered to count."

"Saw you getting out of a cab when I was on deck," Freddie admitted. "He's cute. Always figured he'd have glasses."

"Why?" Mike rolled up his now empty duffle and closed his locker. They had another two hours before they were officially back on duty and he hadn't slept much the night before. He dropped onto the bunk below Freddie's and contemplated a nap.

"You talk about him studying all the time; I got a mental image."

Mike didn't ask whether the cane and Danny's limp had been part of that. It wasn't something he usually mentioned, though he was always at least a little aware of it when they were together. So long after the accident, compensating where Danny needed him to was almost as much second nature for him as it was for Danny. "He doesn't have any jackets with elbow patches. Or geek slogan T-shirts."

Freddie made a noise that could have meant almost anything to someone who hadn't bunked with him for two years. Since Mike had, he knew what that noise meant. "You're picturing him without a shirt right now, aren't you?"

Freddie's head appeared over the side of his bunk, upside down and only faintly repentant around his dark eyes. "He's built, for an academic."

Mike blinked. It didn't do a great deal for the sudden image of Danny and Freddie together. Freddie was tanned, like Mike, in sharp contrast to Danny's pale skin and freckles, and had a good foot of height on Danny. They'd look good together, Mike thought, Freddie on his knees sucking Danny off, Danny's hands trying and failing to grip Freddie's even-shorter-than-regulation dark hair while Freddie's eyes went nearly black with how turned on he was. Or, even better, Freddie prepping Danny for Mike's cock. Freddie didn't have the kind of overt muscles that some military guys had, but there was a sort of clean definition to his body regardless. When he wasn't wearing any clothes, it made every movement very compelling. When he wasn't wearing any clothes and was working Danny open...

"Huh," Mike said intelligently.

Danny would love getting a blow job from Freddie, who had possibly the best mouth of anyone Mike had done that with. Mike stuck himself into the fantasy, curled behind Danny where he was sitting on the bed, rubbing his dick against the small of Danny's back, smudging precome over the smooth skin there as Danny gasped and Freddie did that thing with his tongue that had made Mike's vision go fuzzy, the first time Freddie had done it.

Freddie cleared his throat very pointedly. "You want me to give you a minute?"

When Mike looked up, Freddie was checking out the bulge in his pants. "No," Mike said, letting his hand drift down to rest against his semi-hard dick. "I want you to give me a hand with this."

"Jesus," Freddie groaned, not looking away. "I don't know

whether I'm more bothered by your terrible lines or by the fact that you're trying to get me into your bed after spending a week fucking your hot friend."

Mike very carefully didn't tease—Freddie had the worst luck with men, something that he preferred to talk about only when he was very drunk. "Which one is more likely to help persuade you to get me off?"

"Well, when you put it that way..." Freddie rolled his eyes, but he did it while he was swinging down into Mike's bunk, so Mike didn't call him on it. "You want me to suck you off?" Freddie asked.

Mike's dick twitched in his uniform pants. "Will you do it on your knees?"

Freddie didn't answer, just slid down to his knees and reached for Mike's fly. Mike patted his head a little, but the angle was awkward. "Hold on."

Freddie leaned backward, one hand on the floor behind him. It pushed his hips up, distracting Mike for a moment. He really was hot, especially on his knees in his uniform. Mike dropped his left foot to the floor, giving Freddie room to get his hands onto Mike's thighs, ducking his head to breathe warmly over Mike's cock.

Mike made a low noise in the back of his throat, resting his hand on the back of Freddie's head again. "That's nice."

Freddie huffed a low laugh. "Gonna be better than nice," he promised, and pulled Mike's cock out of his underwear. His hand was dry and cool on Mike. "You got a condom?"

Mike blinked, swallowed down the first words in his head, that he'd used them all up with Danny. It was true, but not exactly tactful. "Do you?"

"No." Freddie huffed out a breath that did approximately nothing for how turned on Mike was. "Maybe I could—"

Freddie pushed into a crouch like he was meaning to stand.

Before he could, Mike caught his shoulder, tugging. Freddie half-caught himself on the edge of Mike's bunk, then, when Mike tugged again, tipped forward to sprawl over him. Both of them groaned at the press of their bodies together, and Mike took advantage of their new proximity to kiss Freddie, putting a little teeth into it so that Freddie gasped. "Take your pants off."

"Yes, sir." Freddie pushed himself up, only just avoiding hitting his head on the underside of the top bunk. "Um."

Mike laughed a little, pressing another kiss to Freddie's neck so he wouldn't be offended. "Maybe let me do it."

Freddie shifted his weight until he was in something more like a push-up. Mike took a moment to just admire how he looked doing it, before fumbling at Freddie's pants. He was already hard, maybe from talking about Danny, maybe from being on his knees for Mike.

"Gonna hold that position?"

"Hell, no." Freddie dropped out of the push-up, but carefully, so his full weight didn't land on Mike. "Now what?"

Mike didn't bother to answer, just got his hand around both their cocks, stroking firmly. "Yeah?"

Freddie snuggled closer, mouthing at Mike's neck above the collar of his shirt. "Yeah."

The first few strokes weren't quite right, too dry, but getting off on a ship full of people meant learning how to do it quickly. It didn't take long before they were leaking against each other, Mike's hand slick as he worked both of them. Freddie rolled his hips into their hands, his breath huffing against Mike's neck. Mike was pretty sure they were going to regret doing this while fully dressed, but he was equally sure that he didn't really care.

"You close?"

"Yeah," Freddie said, sounding almost sleepy. "Yeah, close."

Mike squeezed, gasping a little at how good it felt, Freddie's dick against his. Even with Freddie's words, the first pulse of come over his fingers was a surprise, warm and slick and— "Fuck," he groaned against Freddie's hair as his own orgasm washed over him like an echo of Freddie's.

Unfortunately, he'd been right: hot and sticky was great for about thirty seconds, and then he was mostly dressed with come on his pants and the blanket scratchy against his bare skin. "Ugh."

"Yeah, that's what a guy wants to hear," Freddie said, but he was already climbing to his feet and reaching for a towel. "Come on, before the others rock up."

"So much for the moment," Mike grumbled, swinging his right foot down to join his left, but he was smiling, and the thought of sailing away from Danny wasn't as bad as it had been.

Still on 4 Pride? Mike texted Danny, while trying to come up with a way to explain in the report how his team had ended up nearly drowning during an exercise.

It took Danny fifty-three minutes to text back, which probably meant he'd been in class. *Yes, if you promise not to wear your uniform.* Mike only rolled his eyes a little bit at the way Danny always texted in full, perfectly grammatical sentences, which Danny said was on account of being in academia, and Mike said was on account of not being able to figure out the acronyms.

U think im hot in my uniform. At least, Mike assumed that was why Danny'd talked him into having sex while wearing it. The buttons against Danny's bare skin couldn't have been comfortable.

Why do you think I'm making you promise?

Mike hesitated, turning the phone end over end twice. On his screen, the cursor blinked a reminder that he was supposed to be finishing the damn report, not engaging in fairly pornographic fantasies of his two closest friends. *Thought id ask Freddie if he wants 2 come w/,* he texted eventually. That was probably vague enough.

Tell me what you're planning before I say yes or no.

Or not. Danny knew him way too well not to be suspicious.

U'll like him, he'll like u, Mike sent. Then, in case Danny somehow got the wrong idea, *I like both of u.*

The pause was long enough after that for Mike to check the clock, wondering if Danny could have gone back into class already. No, it was three thirty, and he finished early on Thursdays.

You are exactly what the conservatives were worried about when the repeal went through, Danny texted back eventually, with a smiling face to take the sting out of the remark. Mike was pretty sure the conservatives had actually been worried about gay soldiers seducing their straight teammates over to the rainbow side, but thinking about that stuff still made his heart ache. *Ask me again when I've met him.*

Mike sent back his own smiling face, knowing the sound of Danny capitulating, even if it was just in a text message.

"So, tell me again why I'm here." Freddie frowned at the crowds of people, the rainbow flags and glitter adorning every available surface. The noise was more than Mike could ever remember at Pride, shouting and music and those damn noise-makers going off in his ear, but the contact high he was pretty sure he was getting just by walking down the street made it a lot less painful than it could have been. "The decorating scheme could use a little work."

Mike stopped and stared, as much as he could in the crowd. It wasn't like he never saw Freddie out of his uniform, but he still got a weird little jolt of surprise every time he looked at Freddie. Which may, in fairness, have been because Freddie was wearing a very tight pair of dark blue jeans, the kind that showed off every line and curve. Of course, because he was Freddie, he was wearing a checked shirt over a loose white T-shirt and his uniform boots, but the jeans were a pretty good concession to the event. Mike was probably embodying the stereotypes enough for the both of them, in well-fitted black pants and a tight white T-shirt, hair gelled like he never bothered on ship. "I can't tell if that comment makes you so incredibly gay you should bleed rainbows, or if it makes you the least gay person I know. Who doesn't like rainbows and glitter?"

Freddie shrugged, hunching slightly like that would help him hide in the post-parade chaos, awkward being out in the gay community in a way that he wasn't on the ship. "I'm not sure I've ever been asked to have a personal opinion one way or the other."

"Yeah, well—" Mike caught Freddie's arm, finally spotting the bar Danny had said to meet at. Trust the Navy to run late the one time he had somewhere to be; he couldn't believe he'd missed the parade, it was the best part of Pride. "I'm asking you to have one now, and it had better be that you want to get naked and drape yourself in them."

"I don't think 'drape' is the right verb for glitter," Freddie said, mock-seriously. "Also, if I'm naked, it's going to get in some damn awkward places."

"Rainbow tattoos," Mike told him. "More than one, and glitter nail polish. Even on your toes."

Freddie pressed too close, arms going tight around Mike's waist, pulling him back against Freddie's solid body. Mike tipped his head up without thinking about it, his breath coming short. Even lost in the crowd, made anonymous by all the people around them, this felt dangerous and obvious, sending a burst of arousal through his veins. "I've always been more of a glitter eye shadow person," Freddie said, close enough for Mike to feel his breath. "But whatever works for you."

"That"—Mike cleared his throat—"That really, really works for me."

Freddie stepped away before Mike could say anything else. His grin was smug and pleased, and Mike had no idea why so many good guys overlooked Freddie when he looked like that. "Buy me some, and I'll wear it to the company Christmas party. Come on, your friend will be wondering where we are."

"So, he's the bunk-mate," Danny said, when Freddie excused himself to use the men's room.

Mike glanced in the direction Freddie had gone, though there were way too many people to see him. He figured Danny had picked the bar for its selection of microbrews, or maybe because the chairs actually had backs he could lean into. Either that or he'd picked it because there wasn't a twelve-song club mix playing loud enough to do permanent damage. He sure as hell hadn't picked it for the quiet, not with what felt like half the gay men of San Francisco packed in with them, all trying to communicate by yelling, and an occasional holler.

"He's the bunk-mate," Mike agreed, leaning in so he didn't have to join the general shouting.

Danny made a small, considering noise that Mike could barely hear. He and Freddie had eyed each other suspiciously for the first ten minutes after Mike introduced them. It had been just long enough for Mike to decide this had been a huge mistake, and that he likely wasn't going to be getting any sex at all tonight, let alone sex of the hot threesome variety. Then Danny had mentioned his freshman engineering class, and Freddie had said something about working in his father's garage as a teenager, and that had been the end of Mike's involvement in the conversation as they geeked out over cars and engines like the total nerds they both were.

"Taller than I thought he'd be."

"I showed you a picture."

"Taller in person, then." Danny shrugged. "I like him."

"Told you so."

Danny kicked his ankle. "Don't be smug, it doesn't suit you."

"I brought you home the best present ever; I deserve to be a little bit smug."

Danny's expression went weird, somewhere between charmed and faintly irritated, with something else mixed in that Mike found hard to read. Danny reached over, one hand covering Mike's. Mike couldn't quite make himself hold Danny's hand; he held Danny's gaze instead, waiting. "You'll always be the best present I can have," Danny said, completely serious. "You don't ever have to bring anything else."

It sounded closer to a declaration than they'd ever made. Mike smiled, uncertain. "But an extra present is always good, right?"

The words broke whatever moment they'd been having, and Danny laughed, letting it go. "Sure. An extra present works."

"Tell me you're not talking about Christmas already." Freddie made a face as he threw himself back into the third chair, narrowly avoiding tipping it completely when someone bumped into him. "It's way too early."

"Never hurts to be prepared." Mike spun his empty bottle once between his hands, careful not to send the rest of the empties flying.

"We're not talking about Christmas," Danny said firmly, draining his own beer. "Come on, let's get out of here."

"You want to find a quieter place?" Freddie kept one hand near Danny as they both stood, but didn't grab for him the way some people did in crowds. It got him a grateful look from Danny that made Freddie smile, small and pleased.

Danny shook his head. "Thinking about heading home." He looked over at Mike with the words, checking in about the evening, about Freddie. Mike nodded back; Danny had really been the only wild card in this situation.

"Right," Freddie said, all of the humor and warmth gone from his voice. Even his shoulders were slumping again. "I should—you think I'll get a cab back to the ship somewhere near here?"

Danny frowned at him, and Mike felt the tension ratchet back up, not in a good way. He'd been so sure about Freddie. "Look, no, don't—" Mike started.

"Just—" Danny interrupted him with a sharp hand gesture to Mike without looking away from Freddie. "Mike's an idiot," he said, so softly that Mike was amazed he could hear the words over the roar of conversation in the bar. Danny was smiling though, so something must have been going right again.

Danny grabbed Mike's wrist, pulling him close, the edge of the table digging awkwardly into Mike's hip. "For the record," Danny said, still looking at Freddie, who seemed as confused as Mike felt, "Next time you decide to invite one of your ship-mates into a threesome, it would probably be a good idea to actually invite him."

"I did!" Okay, that had come out a little high-pitched. Mike tried again. "I said, 'Come to Pride with me and Danny.' Did I not say that?"

Freddie's eyes went wide, then closed for a moment, the way they did when he got a particularly ridiculous order. "That was supposed to imply, 'And then come home and have sex with us both?' Yeah, I'm with Danny here. You way undershot the invitation part of that invitation."

"Hopeless," Danny said, voice warm with affection, and okay, *maybe* the two of them had a bit of a point. Apparently Mike had been too subtle. "So, Freddie, in the interests of reducing the amount of inanity going forward: would you like to come back to my apartment and have sex with me and Mike?"

Freddie looked between the two of them, then down to where Danny was still gripping Mike's wrist. "If this is just because of the last guy I hooked up with," he started.

"For the love of—" Danny let go of Mike, shifted his grip on his cane, then leaned in to wrap a hand in Freddie's shirt. "Let me make this very clear," he said, and dragged Freddie down into a harsh kiss.

Freddie's hands flailed for a moment, then settled lightly on Danny's hips. He tilted his head slightly, deepening the kiss. Somewhere in the crowd, someone wolf-whistled. Mike kind of wanted to echo the sentiment. The two of them were exactly as hot together as he'd imagined, and this was while they were still wearing clothes. He was pretty sure the sight of them both naked would lead to spontaneous human combustion, especially given the way Danny always relaxed completely into the first few minutes of being naked and in bed, not worried about his leg and his balance.

Mike was totally willing to risk human combustion for that.

Danny and Freddie drew apart slowly, grinning dumbly at each other. "Yes?" Danny asked.

"Yes," Freddie said. "Oh, most definitely yes."

"So," Mike said, when the three of them were standing in the doorway to Danny's bedroom, shoes and jackets discarded in the living room, glasses of water politely offered and refused. Danny hadn't turned on any lights, just left the curtains open, so the streetlamps cast a weird, orange glow over the neatly made bed and orderly bookshelves. It felt far more intimate than Mike would have expected, especially with the street noise muffled by the windows. "How exactly are we going to do this?"

"You didn't think about that already?" Danny rolled his eyes before Mike could answer. "What am I saying; you didn't actually tell Freddie why he was meeting up with me, of course you didn't think about the actual mechanics of the successful outcome."

Mike put a hand on Danny's waist, then stepped in close enough to wrap his arms around Danny, anchoring him against Mike's body. The whole move took less than ten seconds, which was till ten seconds longer than he wanted to wait before nuzzling Danny's neck and saying, "I love it when you get all forceful."

Danny laughed, sounding as utterly relaxed as Mike felt. Freddie had been designated safe since practically the moment they met, but like this, about to get naked with him and Danny, Mike felt like the last of the fear of being outed and thrown out of the Navy was physically lifting away from him. Freddie, leaning in the doorway and watching the two of them, looked like maybe he'd understand that as well, if Mike said anything.

"We're going to take our clothes off," Danny said, making no move to do so. "Because there is no sexy way to get three full-grown men naked on a double bed."

"Speaking from experience?" Mike teased.

Danny turned his head enough for Mike to see his quirked eyebrow. "Wouldn't you like to know?"

Mike hesitated, caught between two polar opposite answers.

Danny continued before he could decide on one. "Then I'm going to lie back, and Mike's going to ride my cock."

Mike made a small noise, totally unable to contain it. Somehow, Danny's matter-of-fact tone was more of a turn-on than any attempt at sultriness.

"Freddie's going to suck Mike's cock, and I'm going to suck his."

Mike glanced over at Freddie, who was watching them with greedy eyes, then down at Danny, who was visibly turned on by what he was saying. "Good thing you're an engineer," he said.

As it turned out, even the combined spatial awareness of an engineering doctoral student, a sailor with a background in car mechanics and a sailor who specialized in navigation wasn't quite enough to avoid a few elbows and knees in awkward places, or a couple of moments of wrecked rhythm. About the best that could be said for them, honestly, was that they didn't manage to jolt Danny in any way that would hurt enough to lose the moment.

When they finally got it figured out, though, it was totally worth the bruises. Mike couldn't work himself on Danny's cock the way he usually did, not when Freddie's mouth was on him at the same time, but the roll of his hips, Danny deep inside him, was a whole other order of intense pleasure. Freddie was tentative at first, moving in tiny jerks of his hips, obviously uncertain of his welcome.

Mike reached down, smoothing a hand over the defined lines in the backs of Freddie's shoulders. He meant it to be soothing, but it made Freddie moan around his cock, and Mike had to do it again. Freddie's skin was so warm under his hands, damp with sweat already. Mike bent low. "He can take it. Come on, Freddie."

Freddie shuddered all over, but his next move was smoother. He dug his feet into the mattress, ass flexing as he rocked into Danny's mouth, Danny groaning around his cock like it was the best thing ever.

"You look so good like this," Mike told Freddie, resting one hand on the back of his neck to feel the way his muscles shifted as he moved. "Your mouth is—fuck, amazing. So good." Freddie didn't say anything, which wasn't a surprise at all; he was always near silent during sex, even when his mouth wasn't full of cock. "Are you sucking me the way Danny's sucking you? I bet you are. He's so good at this, man, you don't even— taught me everything I know about sucking cock, Danny, you're so—"

Mike bit his lip, words he didn't say clamoring in the back of his throat. He couldn't say them, not like this; not when he wasn't even sure who he'd be saying them to, pinned between the two people he cared most for in the world, loving every second of it.

"You're so good," he said instead, low and soft in the darkness. "You're perfect."

No one said anything at all after that, too intent on driving each other to climax, spiraling up and up on the smell of sex and sweat, the sound of harsh breathing and skin rubbing against skin. Freddie came first, shuddering hard and pulling off Mike's cock to gasp for breath.

Mike moaned, reaching for him, pulling him back. Freddie

cried out—probably Danny doing that thing with his tongue that he did when Mike was almost done coming, that made him feel like he was having his orgasm all over again—and Mike took advantage of it, dragging Freddie's mouth back to his cock. "Don't stop, so close," he managed, not even caring whether Freddie was really sucking him anymore, and then Freddie slid a hand back to rub at the place where Mike was sinking down onto Danny's cock.

It was more than enough to tip Mike over the edge. He heard Danny keen something sharp and cracking as he went over, felt Danny's cock pulse inside him, but he was already mostly gone, swept up by pleasure.

He came back to himself to find he hadn't collapsed on anyone like he'd thought, but also that his thighs ached from kneeling for way too long. He winced as he climbed off Danny, Freddie wisely sliding off the bed as he did so. Danny looked most of the way to sleep, which was pretty unusual; whatever it was that made most guys pass out after sex, Danny didn't have it. He was soft-eyed now, though, watching Freddie and Mike from under lowered eyelashes.

Mike grabbed a spare shirt to clumsily clean himself and Danny up. Freddie took it from him when he finished, looking like he was planning on making a trip to the bathroom. Mike caught his arm before he could and pulled Freddie down for a kiss. Freddie's mouth tasted familiar, like every blow job they'd shared in the Navy.

"No more sex now," Danny said, the command totally lost to the slow drawl of his voice. "Sleep now."

"I don't know that this bed is made for three people," Freddie said doubtfully.

"Sure it is." Mike flopped down, tugging on Freddie's arm enough to make the intention clear, but not so much that he'd fall on any of Danny's damaged parts. Freddie took the hint, and they wound up on either side of Danny, pressing close. After a long moment, Freddie pulled the covers over them all.

"See?" Mike asked.

"Whatever," Danny said. "Sleep now. Sex in the morning. And waffles."

"Coffee," Freddie added. "I know a place."

And kisses, Mike thought as he slipped down into sleep. He didn't say it, but that didn't matter; he didn't need to say it to know that he'd get to have them. That they all would.

LIBERTY

Dominic Santi

Ninety-six hours of liberty. Damn, I was looking forward to it. I slid my palm over the identilock and walked into the barracks room, dropping my web gear on the chair as the door closed behind me. After seven days in the field, I was tired, I stank and I was so horny all I could think about was burying myself balls deep up Eric's ass.

My hunky husband was already home, holding the com unit to his ear as he unlaced his scuffed, muddy boots. Eric was as dirty as I was, his short blond hair plastered to his head and his usually pristine utilities stiff with grime. But when he smiled up at me, his sparkling gray eyes lit his whole face. I grinned back like a fool. I knew I looked like hell. The dark curls matted to my scalp itched as much as my balls did. All I could think about, though, was how good Eric's firm, compact body was going to look when he'd stripped down to his skin and his thick, heavy cock was arching up toward his washboard abs. Eric and I are both short and muscular—we pride ourselves on staying toned even under the lousiest conditions. My cock filled as I thought about the great workout I was going to give his ass, and vice versa, as soon as he got off the house com and we'd cleaned up enough to kiss.

Before I could settle in to really admire the scenery, though, Eric said, "Caleb just walked in the door. Let me get him for you."

The way Eric danced past should have warned me. I picked up the receiver to hear, "I want grandchildren!"

I turned and gave Eric the dirtiest look I could, mouthing the words, *You asshole!* as he grinned and ducked into the fresher. Our last weekend before we jumped—I did not want to spend it arguing with my mother, again, on what was fast becoming her favorite topic.

"We have plenty of time, Mom. Eric and I haven't even been married the two-year minimum for surrogacy..."

She wasn't buying it. She'd figured out every innuendo of the military exemptions way faster than I'd ever dreamed she could. Not that I really blamed her. Both my family and Eric's had been decimated by the enviro-plagues of the late twenty-first century. We were only sons. We had compatible first-degree surrogates—my sister, his youngest aunt. And Eric and I were combat infantry NCOs.

I knew my mother loved me to distraction, but she was also terrified of losing my genotypes before I'd reproduced. While the tide of the Bashari war had finally turned in Earth's favor, the fighting was far from over. Eric and I had both been wounded in the battle for Tartrioch. Now that we'd healed, even our families knew our dirtside tour to learn the newest weapon technology was short-term.

Still, I was tired of the nagging. These days, the whole topic made me uncomfortable. I put my brain on autopilot, peeling out of my clothes and kicking them into the corner. I concentrated on scratching my blissfully freed balls and thinking about how Eric would look when he stepped back into the room.

He didn't disappoint me. He was still wet from his cleaning. I felt the familiar tug of love and lust as I looked at the lightly furred expanse of muscular, naked thigh peeking out from under his loosely knotted towel. The skin-hugging cloth that emphasized the perfect curve of his ass was nowhere near big enough to hide the erection tenting out in front of him. Eric always played with himself in the fresher—not enough to make himself come on a night we both had off, but enough to get himself good and horny. My own dick twitched in response.

"Caleb, are you listening to me?" The exasperated voice in the com unit drew me back from my lust-filled reverie. "What if, god forbid, something happened to you—or to Eric! You have to do something about this!"

"There's time," I muttered, trying to ignore the interruption as my thoughts fixated on exactly what I wanted to do with my lover. But just then Eric turned. Once again, my gut lurched at the sight of the long, jagged, angry-red scar that stretched from his kidney halfway up his back. I looked away, concentrating hard on how he was so alive now, so sexy—and obviously slightly pissed as he picked up my dirty clothes, holding them at arm's length as he stuffed them down the laundry tube with the neat bundle he'd carried from the other room.

"Caleb, please..."

"I'll think about it!" I snapped, rattled that the memories had shaken me again. "I have to go. I'll call you Monday night, before we jump."

There was dead silence on the line.

"Ah, shit," I muttered. "I'm sorry." Eric and I had been

talking about the jump all week. I'd forgotten we hadn't been cleared to tell family until tonight.

"That soon." There was a moment more of silence, then a quiet, "Just remember, we love you both. Give Eric a hug for us."

"We love you, too." I had to smile. It was hard to stay mad at somebody who was saying things like that. "And don't worry, okay? Eric and I—we'll talk about it."

I set the com unit down slowly and turned back to watch Eric. He was sitting at the desk chair now, the floor around him covered with drop cloths, his shoulders rippling softly as he polished our boots and brass. He was much more meticulous than I was. I didn't mind a ding or two, especially in the field. Eric minded. Now that we were back home, he was, as usual, getting both our gear back up to his standards of presentability. When he saw me looking at him, he shrugged and spat on my boot.

"For this, I expect dinner, pal."

I grabbed my crotch and forced myself to grin back. "Come and get it, stud."

"That's dessert." He wiggled his eyebrows as he went back to polishing. "Or maybe an appetizer." He nodded toward the com, his tone telling me he wasn't buying my "everything's okay" act. "Still the same topic?"

"Yeah," I sighed, walking over to stand next to him. It was such a relief to be married to somebody I could be honest with. "I get so tired of the nagging." I took a deep breath, watching him closely as I leaned against the wall. "She does have a point, though."

Eric stopped rubbing long enough to stare up at me. I blushed. In reality, I'd been the one who had hesitated about having children, insisting we enjoy a long honeymoon before we settled down. These days, though, I wasn't feeling quite as immortal as I used to.

"I've been thinking about it." I ran my fingers lightly over his shoulder. "All we have to do is come in a collection tube. They can run the viral filters and freeze it so the gestation coincides with our next Earthside tour, after the war. And if something happens…" I stopped as my stomach lurched. I didn't want to think about that.

"What if something happens?" Eric's voice was quiet as he reached up and brushed his fingertips over the line of scars across my chest. They only hurt deep inside now, but the difference in the way my skin responded to his touch was a constant reminder to both of us of what each jump could mean. "We've always talked about raising our family together." Eric's hand stilled as his laughing gray eyes for once turned serious. "Would you want all that responsibility by yourself?"

"Yes." It was an instinctive response, but something deep inside me seemed to slide into place as I realized that no matter what, I wanted there to be children, somewhere, who were a mixture of our genes. The whole idea still terrified me, but I wanted it. I took Eric's hand and squeezed hard.

"What about you?"

Eric's grin lit his face. I'd known since I'd met him that being a dad was one of the biggest priorities in his life. "Oh, yeah, Caleb. Just the thought of shooting into that sheath makes me hard. We're going to be great parents." He leaned over and licked my nipple. "You real sore, or can I chew for a while?"

"Go ahead," I nodded, shivering as his tongue trailed over my pecs. "You know, though, we can't come for forty-eight hours before we make the donation." I gasped as he teethed lightly on my suddenly rock-hard nipple. The pain was only a distant, dull ache, overshadowed by the tingling pleasure of his sharp kisses. "We could hold off and do it in the morning."

"No way," he laughed. My cock twitched as his hand slid down and cupped my balls. "I've been hungry for your dick all week, pal. Those poor unhappy sperm cells in here are getting weak from lack of action." He tugged lightly on my sac as his breath whispered over my wet nipple. "I'm going to suck you and fuck you and ride your dick until you're cleared wide open for the biggest, freshest, strongest load of baby-making swimmers you've ever shot. You're going to drain your balls coming in that sheath, lover. And you're going to make me do the same." He licked my tit one last time, squeezing my crotch as my boner reached for his hand. "Now get in that fresher. You stink, and I really want to fuck you."

It didn't take me long to get clean, but after a week of wearing the same sweat, I stayed in the fresher a while longer, enjoying the luxury of hot synthetic water. Eric got tired of waiting, so he sat down under my balls and "helped" me finish up, polishing my dick and asshole with his tongue until we were too turned on to even think about getting dressed that night. I ordered a pizza and we spent the rest of the night fucking each other senseless.

The next morning, we threw ourselves into a flurry of finishing up personal business and putting the few possessions we bothered to keep into storage. As usual, Eric and I were being assigned to the same unit. The military did its best to keep married couples together. I felt a strange sense of intimacy, of wanting to touch Eric all the time, as we once more closed up our household. Just the thought that we were actually going to do it—we were going to make babies and plan for a settled future—had me feeling embarrassingly romantic, and constantly horny, and scared shitless.

Two days later, we were at the clinic. The surrogacy donation rooms were homey—large, comfortable beds with lots of pillows, soft lighting and a state of the art sound system for the classical background music we'd chosen. All of which belied the medical precision of what we were doing. The surrogacy programs weren't hit or miss anymore. By the time Eric and I were back on Earth again, the first of our children would be ready to be born.

"Looks like the two of you will be mixing some primo genes." The smirking, dark-haired technician was the type of sculpted eye-candy clinics employed to stimulate those who needed a kick start beyond the stacks of porn and sex toys on the nightstand. Eric and I stripped naked under his watchful and obviously interested eyes. Once we'd cleaned up and disinfected, the tech showed us how to use the collection sheaths, rolling one of the thin, transparent polyskins over a dildo and securing the sealant into place.

"Be sure it's tight," he said, running his finger around the edge to be sure there were no leaks. "You need to capture as much as possible of your preseminal fluid as well as your ejaculate. And don't be surprised when the lube inside turns white. It's a nutrient preservative to keep your sperm healthy. It'll feel cool at first, but it will warm to body temperature as soon as it starts reacting to your fluids."

After a couple of practice runs with the dildo, he seemed convinced we knew how to use the sheaths properly. With one final, lecherous grin toward our crotches, he gathered up his clipboard. "Remember, DO NOT mix up your donations. I'll be at the desk down the hall. Press the buzzer over the bed when you're done." He closed the door behind himself, and Eric and I were alone.

"I can't believe we're here," Eric said, laughing as he pulled me to him in a tight bear hug. "Jeez, I love you. And I'm so fucking horny. Let's make us some babies."

I was so nervous my dick couldn't decide if it wanted to get hard or shrivel up, so I stretched out on the bed and held my arms out to him. Though the clinic recommended we use dildos to stimulate our prostate glands, we were going to do things the old-fashioned way—by fucking each other. We'd decided I'd go first, because after a few days of deprivation, I can almost always get it up a second time, no matter how hard I shoot the first. Eric had the staying power to fuck me into shooting while holding back long enough for me to do the same for him. And we were going to do it face-to-face, so we could kiss and hug—and watch each other come.

Fortunately, just knowing Eric was going to fuck me got my motor running. By the time we stopped kissing enough to come up for air, my dick was climbing toward my belly. Eric stuffed a couple of pillows under my hips as I tipped back and lifted my legs. I stroked myself a few times to be sure I was hard enough. Then I slipped the sheath over the head of my dick and pressed the seal into place. My cock twitched in anticipation as I slid the cool, nutrient-slicked covering back and forth.

"Oh, man, you look so hot," Eric whispered. His eyes shone almost silver as he cupped my sac in his hand, rolling my balls one at a time between his warm, strong fingers. "Your nuts feel so full."

My dick grew even harder as Eric leaned over and tenderly kissed the back of my knee. His tongue swirled up my leg until he was sucking softly at the sensitive flesh where my thigh joined my ass. His tongue traced the outline of my scrotum, nuzzling and kissing and washing me with his hot spit. Then his cheeks pressed against the sides of my crack, and his tongue teased over my sphincter.

"Oh yeah," I gasped. I couldn't help arching up against him.

"You taste good." Eric's breath was cool as it slid past my

spit-slicked asshole. "I'm going to get you nice and wet, lover. I'm going to eat you until your hole is loose and open and reaching for me, then I'm going to fuck every last sperm cell out of your body. You're going to see stars, babe."

Nobody, and I mean nobody, eats ass like Eric does. He dug in and tongue-fucked me until I thought I was going to lose my mind. I felt like an animal in heat, squirming and moaning and holding his head to me as my whole body pressed up and begged him to fuck me. I could feel my asshole opening for him, reaching to kiss him back, quivering each time his voice reverberated through me.

"You're almost ready, baby," he murmured as I shook beneath him. I groaned as his fingers spread me even wider and his tongue slid in deeper. "Mmmm. I love the way your butt kisses me back." His shoulders rippled as he stroked himself with his other hand. "Open for me, honey. I'm going to make you feel so good." His finger tickled over my prostate. I cried out as my whole body shuddered. "Yeah," he laughed. "Just like that."

I was gasping by the time he rose up over me.

"This is it," Eric whispered. He leaned down and kissed me. "I'm going to fuck you now. Going to push every one of those little fuckers right up out of you. You're going to come so hard your toes will curl. You got that, lover?" His tongue tasted musky and faintly of soap as he licked the inside of my lips. "You're going drain your balls on this come. Right...now!"

I cried out as he sank into me. My sphincter tensed for just the slightest moment, then it gave way and I sucked him in almost to his balls. I closed my eyes, stroking slowly over my encased dick as I groaned with pleasure.

"Get ready for a long, hard fuck, lover." Eric lifted up onto his arms, his cock sliding almost all the way out then plunging back in again. I moaned as he pressed hard against my joyspot. "I can see your precum seeping into the sheath, Caleb. The fluid's turned all milky. I bet you'll keep leaking, the way you always do when I'm fucking you deep and hard."

I could feel the hot juice oozing through my cocktube. Eric's chest glistened with sweat as he raised and lowered his gorgeous body over mine, his thick, heavy cock sliding slowly and sensuously over my hypersensitive asslips. I knew I wouldn't last long. He was hitting my joyspot with each thrust. I could feel the orgasm building deep inside.

"Harder," I gasped. I shuddered as he pressed my legs even farther back, grinding against my prostate. "Oh fuck, yeah!"

I wrapped my hand around my dick, the stimulation on my quivering shaft almost more than I could stand. I stroked furiously in time to Eric's thrusting. My body was drawing in on itself, my nuts climbing my shaft as my guts clenched around his cock. Eric was smiling so big it looked like his face would split.

"Let it happen, babe. Let your cocktube open so wide every last one of those suckers comes shooting out like a cannon ball." He started rabbit-thrusting. My cock tensed rock hard into my hand.

"Gonna come," I gasped. Eric's panting filled my ears. He pressed deep and hard, grinding against my joyspot. My ass clamped down around his thick, hot cock. I stroked again, my hand sliding slick and tight over my throbbing dickhead as my cock started spurting. I yelled as the long, slow, body-draining pulses emptied my balls all the way to my spine.

I was still shaking, trying to breathe, when I looked up to see Eric frozen above me, his whole body stiff as he took deep, trembling breaths.

"Don't move," he gasped. "Or I'll shoot. God, you're so tight, Caleb. Your ass is so sweet." Eric's face was flushed a deep, dick red. I could almost see the blood throbbing through the veins in his neck. I willed my asshole to relax, to not grip and milk the throbbing cock buried in my ass.

Eric withdrew slowly, panting as he crawled back from the edge. I peeled off my container, sealing it and marking it with my thumbprint before I set the still-warm polyskin on the tray beside the bed. Eric was dripping sweat as he again wiped his dick down with disinfectant and carefully rolled his sheath down his shaft. The fluid turned milky instantly as his precum dripped into the receptacle.

"I'm not going to last long," Eric gasped as he rolled over onto his back. He pulled his knees up and back, his rock-hard dick arching up over his belly.

"Don't touch my cock," he panted as I buried my face in his crack. "I'm too close." He groaned out loud as I swiped my tongue between his open cheeks and started tonguing his sweet, tight sphincter. He was sweaty all over now, his ass thick with the scent of his musk in spite of the soap and disinfectant. I bent him farther back, opening his hole to my probing. He wiggled and gasped, heat radiating out of him as I licked the edges of his asslips, kissing harder, poking my tongue in deeper. I spread his asscheeks wide, grinning as his sphincter gave way and my lips pressed up hard against his pucker.

"Fuck, your tongue feels good!" Eric was writhing beneath me. He grabbed my hair in a death grip, grunting as he arched his ass up toward me. I sucked his asslips in a long, slow, wet kiss. His hole was as ready as a boy's could be.

"I can't hold off much longer," he gasped. "My balls are churning. Fuck me, Caleb. Now—please!"

I was so wasted from my climax I'd been afraid I'd have to use a dildo after all. But watching Eric so totally out of control kept me hard while I humped the mattress. I started lubing him up, stretching him with my fingers as I rubbed his hypersensitive ball sac with my thumbs.

"You're ripe, babe," I whispered, massaging each orb, handling them as gently as near-bursting seed pods while I worked his asshole open the rest of the way. A pool of white juices filled the tip of his collection sheath. "Your balls are ready to explode, lover."

"Please, Caleb," Eric whispered. He shuddered, gasping and arching up as I lightly tickled my finger over his joyspot. "Don't! I want to come while you're fucking me. I want it so bad!"

His cock was drooling almost constantly, his face flushed with lust. He cried out as I started into him, the head of my throbbing cock slowly stretching him.

"Want you," he gasped. He lifted his ass to me, bearing down, his voice keening as I slid up into him. Eric loved a slow fuck. I gave it to him, pressing the precum out of him one drooling strand at a time, mercilessly matching my strokes to his long, quivering pulls on his dick.

"I love you," I whispered. "We're going to make beautiful kids. The best." I dragged almost all the way out then slid back in as slowly as I could. Eric cried out, his heat sliding over my dick like a glove as he started to shake. His sphincter clamped down on me and I jumped in surprise as my own tired dick tensed to come.

"Shoot for me babe," I gasped, willing myself to hold off. Eric was so beautiful, he took my breath away. Then he was yelling, his dick spurting wildly into the sheath as he convulsed beneath me, and my own startled shaft shot almost dry up his ass.

Eric collapsed on the bed, trembling as I carefully peeled off his sheath, sealed it and pressed his thumb to the imprint square. I pushed the buzzer over the bed, then I dragged Eric into my arms and curled up around him. I was asleep before the attendant arrived to pick up the donations. We had the bed for another hour, and like any good soldier, I grabbed my sleep when I could—especially when I was dreaming about the great future Eric and I were going to have together, we and our kids.

A VOICE IN
THE DARK

Neil Plakcy

The male voice came out of the dark. "You speak English?"

I rubbed my wrists where they'd tied me up with rope. It didn't feel like the skin had been broken on either arm, but it was too damn dark in the room to tell. "American. You?"

The voice was rough, as if he had something stuck in his throat. "Seventy-Fifth Ranger Regiment," he said.

"I'm impressed. Regular Army here." My eyes began to get accustomed to the lack of light in the windowless cell, and I made out the shape of another man sitting on the floor across from me. I stepped over and extended my hand downward. "Captain Jeremy Groom, First Infantry."

He didn't stand but shook my hand. "Lieutenant Alec Macpherson."

His grip was strong beneath the ragged bandages that covered his hand, and the warmth of his hand in mine sent an immediate and dangerous message to my groin.

"How long have you been here?" I asked. I looked around, finally able to see where I was. The cell was about eight feet long and four feet wide; the floor was packed earth but the walls were concrete block. No windows. No furniture, just a foul-smelling bucket in the corner in lieu of a toilet.

Summer in the Afghan highlands was ending, and the outside temperature had been in the high sixties. It was warmer inside than it had been outdoors, probably the result of the mountain sun heating the corrugated roof.

I shucked my soft-shell jacket, leaving me in a camo shirt and pants, with wool socks and boots and a light-green T-shirt and boxers underneath.

"What day is it?" Alec asked, as I dropped my jacket to the ground.

"October first."

"Then I've been here about two weeks," he said. "I was captured in the mountains outside this nowhere town called Fayzabad. But then I spent a couple of days tied up in the back of a truck."

"No idea where Fayzabad is," I said. "I got separated from my convoy on a trip from Kabul to Jalalabad."

"You think we're close to Kabul now? Or Jalalabad?"

"Not sure. Like you, I spent a couple of days in a truck."

"So we have no fucking idea where we are."

"Maybe." I sat down across from him. When I'd been pushed out of the back of the truck, I'd seen the building we were in; it was squat and single-story, with front windows that had been boarded up, and a faded sign in Arabic lettering. "When they brought me in I recognized the word for school over the front door," I said. "It was in Dari."

The Dari language, also known as Farsi or Afghan Persian, dominated in the north, western and central parts of the country. It was the lingua franca of Afghanistan, though Pashto dominated in the south.

"You can read it?"

"I'm a tactical linguist. Dari, Pashto and Farsi. Don't you get language training in the Rangers?"

"I can speak a little Dari but can't read shit. How'd you get caught?"

"I was attached to a UN-sponsored mission with family planning information for native women. I was translating at an information session at a village when bombs started flying. I was taken while I was helping some women get away. How about you?"

"Mission failure. Pinned down while providing cover." Alec struggled to sit up against the wall. I could see he was hurt but couldn't tell how badly. "You able to see anything else that might tell us where we are?"

I shrugged. "We're at the base of a mountain. Dusting of snow at the top. Early afternoon when they brought me in."

"Which side of the mountain?"

"West side. We're in kind of a bowl—lower mountains to the north and south. Open plains to the east." I hesitated then figured that very quickly there would be no secrets between us. "How bad are you hurt?"

"I'll survive."

"Cut the bad-boy bravado. Specifics?"

He grunted. "I thought at first that my left ankle was broken, but I can't feel any broken bones, and as long as I don't put pressure on it there isn't much pain." He held up his hands, which were wrapped in grimy cloth. "Knife wounds to both hands. They sting but I think they're healing. Hard to see anything in here."

I looked up. Daylight filtered through a tiny gap where the flat metal roof rested on top of the highest course of concrete block. "Can you stand?" I asked.

"As long as I don't put too much weight on my left side. But the ceiling's low—in some places I have to duck my head an inch or two."

"Perfect. Stand up."

"Why?"

"See that gap up there? If we can make it bigger we'll have a better idea of day and night."

"Tried that already. The concrete's too hard."

"But you didn't have what I do." I reached down and took off my right boot. A month before, the insole had begun separating from the base. Instead of requisitioning a new pair, I had tucked a tiny file with a sharp end into the gap. I reached inside and dug my finger around until I found it.

"Resourceful," Alec said. He struggled to get up, and I grabbed him under one arm to lift. He was a big guy, with powerful biceps. His raw masculinity sent a thrill of desire through my body.

Once he stood, I had a better sense of him. At least six-four, broad shouldered and deep chested, with a narrow waist. His camouflage T-shirt hung loosely, indicating that he'd lost weight in his captivity. I handed him the file, and when our hands touched I felt that electricity again.

The last time I'd gotten laid was on R&R six months before. After Don't Ask, Don't Tell was wiped out, I came out to my commander, and eventually the rest of my team. I was the only gay soldier I knew and even if I'd known another, I was smart enough to keep my dick in my pants when it came to the military.

Alec listed to the right as he tried to keep the weight off his left leg. "I need to turn around," he said. "If I face the wall, I can lean on it."

"All right." I put my hands on his waist, one of them slipping accidentally beneath his T-shirt to the smooth flesh beneath. I flashed back to the last time I'd touched a man's skin, a week before I shipped out, and my dick swelled.

I pulled my hand away and replaced it over his waistband. I helped him turn, steadying him as he hopped on his right foot in a half-circle. He was so close to me I could have leaned forward to kiss the back of his neck. I had to back my hips away so my hard-on didn't press against his ass.

He leaned against the wall, bracing himself with his right foot, and tried to raise his right arm. But he couldn't maintain his balance, and I had to body-block him to keep him upright. I was sure that my hard-on jammed against his butt as I grabbed him, but neither of us mentioned it.

He switched the file to his left hand and raised it to the ceiling. He began to pick at the concrete, and tiny bits flew out of the opening. I could see he was having trouble keeping his arm raised, and I put the flat of my hand beneath his left bicep to hold him up. "Yeah, that's good," he said.

The musky smell of his underarm filled my nostrils as he chipped away at the concrete. "Not too much," I said. "Just enough so we can get some light. But we don't want it too visible to them."

"Not my first time at the rodeo," Alec grunted. My own arm started to flag and I shifted my body so I could keep his arm up. That meant my hard-on was pressing against his butt again. I tried to back away but Alec shifted his ass so I couldn't move.

Huh? Did he know what was going on, or was he just struggling for a better position?

He took out a quarter-sized chunk and real sunlight came into the cell in a thin stream. For the first time I got a good look at him—though from behind. His hair was a dirty blond, his buzz cut starting to grow out. He had a tattoo on his left bicep of interwoven barbed wire.

"I think that's enough for now," he said, and his body sagged as he lowered his arm.

"You should probably sit down," I said, cradling one arm around his back as he lowered himself. As we went down together my face ended up against his, feeling the scratch of his beard against my smooth-shaven cheek.

The first man I ever kissed had a mustache and a soul patch, and ever since then I've had a taste for hairy faces. I wanted nothing more than to rub my cheek against his, luxuriating in the feel of his skin on mine. But I backed off as he slipped down to a sitting position.

He handed me the file and I sat on the rough ground to replace it in my shoe. By the time I was finished he was stretched out on the ground, with his camo jacket balled up under his head as a pillow. "Gonna take a nap," he said. "Wake me when the rapture comes."

"Will do."

I sat back against the wall as Alec nodded off. I didn't think the extra gap would be noticeable to our captors; the hall outside had enough light that their eyes would have to adjust to the darkness inside, as mine had.

I watched Alec sleep, taking note of his smooth forehead and slim eyebrows. He had a broad face with a small nose and wide mouth. Damn, he was handsome, and the multi-day growth of his beard only made him appear more masculine. I didn't see much body hair—nothing around the neck or over his impressive biceps. His pecs were just as big.

But enough horn-dogging. The military had attempted to train me to think logically, so I considered my situation. I was locked in a cell in an isolated area of Afghanistan, held by captors I thought were Taliban—but I wasn't sure. Four men, a mix of teens and adults, had brought me there in the truck, but I didn't know how many had remained.

My cellmate had a weak ankle and appeared to have gotten debilitated during the time of his captivity. The fact that he'd been there for a while implied that they were in no hurry to get rid of either of us.

Our only weapon, as far as I could tell, was the tiny file in my shoe. If I got close enough to a jailer, I might be able to use the file to cut him or even put out an eye. But would that be enough? And was I adept enough to manage? Alec undoubtedly could; Rangers were famous for being able to get out of tough situations with their wits and brawn alone.

The door to the cell swung open and banged against the wall. An elderly Afghan man with a creased face, missing several teeth, held out two two flat ovals of *nan-e Afghani*, the native bread cooked in a tandoori oven. He wore a light-blue headscarf and a woven sweater in a pattern of blue and purple diamonds.

I jumped up and began speaking in rapid Dari. "This man is injured. He needs soap and water and clean bandages. If you don't keep him alive he will die, and you will lose his value as a hostage."

"I am just an old man," he said, thrusting the bread toward me. It was still warm, speckled with tiny burnt circles, and smelled rich and doughy.

I took the bread, and he backed away, slamming the door behind him.

"What did you say to him?" Alec asked.

I handed him one of the flat breads. "That you needed fresh bandages." I took a bite of the bread, which tasted as delicious as anything I'd ever eaten, and I realized how long it had been since I'd had food in my stomach. "This is all we get?"

"There'll be stew later."

"Is he the only one who's ever come to look after you?" I asked.

"As far as I know. I've heard other voices, so there might be more."

I chewed the bread slowly, to make it last, and wished I had some water to go with it. A few minutes later, the cell door swung open again. This time the old man had a basin of water, a bottle of U.S.-issued hand sanitizer and a roll of gauze over his shoulder. He handed the stuff to me without saying anything, then left.

"You must have the magic touch," Alec said.

I shrugged. "It's a gift. Let's see what your hands look like."

He shifted position into the shaft of light, and I began to unwrap the dirty gauze. It could have been worse; his wounds were angry and red, but they had scabbed over and there wasn't evidence of gangrene or any serious infection. "Whoever wrapped you up the first time did a good job," I said, balling up the layers of flimsy gray fabric.

"I did it."

I looked up at him. "You?"

"Rangers learn field medicine. Ninety percent of deaths in the field come from nonfatal wounds left untreated."

His left hand was shaking, and I clasped it in both of mine to calm it.

"That feels good," he said.

His eyes were light blue, the color of the early morning sky. I looked deep into them, then, embarrassed, pulled my hands back. I had learned to keep a clean handkerchief in my pants pocket, and I dug it out, then dipped it in the warm water and wrung it out.

"You don't have to do that," he said, reaching for the cloth. "I can manage."

"You'll cross-contaminate," I said briskly. "If you try and clean one hand with another that's already dirty. Just let me take care of you."

He smiled. "Yes, sir."

I liked his smile. "Good attitude, soldier," I said.

"But if I were you…" he began.

I looked up at him.

"I'd take a drink before getting the water dirty. And I'd give one to my buddy, too. You don't know when the next time we'll see water will be."

"Good idea." I lifted the bowl and took a small sip. The tepid water tasted metallic, but it felt great on my parched throat. We passed the bowl back and forth a couple of times, taking small sips. When we were finished, I carefully wiped away the dirt from his hands, one by one, spraying each with the hand sanitizer. When they were dry I wrapped the bandage around them sparingly, leaving his fingers free to function.

We spent a very intimate half hour together, sitting close to each other, one of us always touching the other. The feel of his skin against mine sent my heart racing and made my dick swell. I felt myself blushing and hurried through the final steps. Then I moved back to my side of the cell.

When things got boring in the field, I often spun myself elaborate fantasies to keep my mind occupied. I'd daydream about running away from the war, for example. Just start walking toward the north, in the direction of the border to Tajikistan, which had so far remained aloof to the Afghan conflict.

I'd imagine how I would survive, finding a river to follow, threading my way through fields and around the bases of mountains. I would glean food as I passed, drinking from rivers, maybe even catching a fish. One summer in high school, I took a two-week outdoor survival course, and combined with what I'd learned in the Army, it made me confident I could manage.

Things got hazier once I reached the border. If I just walked away from my commission, I'd be a deserter, and I wasn't sure how close the Tajik language was to anything I spoke. That was usually where the fantasy faded away.

I looked up to see Alec staring at me. "You looked like you were in your happy place," he said. "Where's that?"

I was embarrassed to be the subject of his scrutiny. "Just walking," I said. "Out in the countryside."

He nodded. "I wish I could walk away sometimes myself. It's crazy, you know? I mean, what are we doing here anyway? The Afghans don't want us. The Talibs certainly don't. We could just pull out and leave them to kill each other."

"And then they'd come after us," I said. "The Talibs don't just want to run this country, they want to wipe out everyone who disagrees with them. All over the world."

"That's the story they tell us," Alec said.

"Let me take a look at your ankle now." I sat cross-legged across from him and lifted his leg gently so that his foot rested in my lap. I unlaced his boot and slipped it off, and he winced.

"Buck up, soldier," I said. He leaned forward to swat me but I shifted out of his reach. I slid the sock off and felt the ankle. "Can you move your toes?"

He wiggled them.

Having his naked foot in my lap was very erotic, and I could feel my dick bouncing back up again. Jesus, was I that much of a horn-dog? I ran my hands gently over his rough sole and the smooth skin above. "The foot doesn't feel that swollen," I said. "Just tender. Hey, does that make you a tenderfoot?"

"It makes you a lot less than a field medic," Alec grumbled.

"But I have to say it feels better out of the boot." He yawned. "Time for another nap."

He pulled his foot back, stretched out on the floor, adjusted his camo jacket beneath his head and closed his eyes.

He looked so handsome in that shaft of light, like a sleeping angel. A very buff, masculine angel, his light green T-shirt riding up to reveal a line of smooth flesh. He rested on his back, and my eyes were drawn to his groin, wondering if his dick would be as big as the rest of him was. I fantasized about sneaking over there while he was asleep, palming his goods through his camo pants, just to get a feel for them.

Then, if he didn't wake, I might get more daring. I'd seen the waistband of his boxers peeking out above his pants. I could unzip those pants, reach through the slit in his boxers and touch him. His dick would be warm and firm, like the rest of him. With a few expert strokes, I could bring his dick to life, using his precum to lubricate my efforts.

And then, what the hell. I'd go down on him, taking that succulent dick in my mouth, teasing him with my tongue, tantalizing him, making his blood race the way mine did when I looked at him.

The thought of it was making me hard. He was still asleep, tiny snores rippling his lips, and I reached down and slowly unzipped my pants, leaving them splayed out over my groin as my stiff dick surged through my boxers. Slowly and quietly, I began to stroke myself.

"You're not just going to torment me, are you?" Alec said, his eyes still closed.

I hurried to stuff my dick back into my pants. "Sorry?"

"You don't have to put it away on my account," he said, sitting up, with a sly grin on his face.

"I wasn't...I mean, I didn't..."

"You were jacking yourself off," he said, resting his right hand over his groin so I couldn't see if he was hard or not. "It's all right. Guys do it all the time."

He shifted position and I saw his hard-on poking against his pants. "What's your fantasy?" he asked. "You have a girl back home you were thinking of?"

I shook my head, licking my dry lips. I took a deep breath and said, "I'm gay."

He laughed. "No shit, Sherlock. I knew the first time you rubbed your woody against my ass."

"I wasn't rubbing it!" I said indignantly.

"Sure you were. Made me hard when you did. Or didn't you notice?"

"You?"

"Queer as a three-dollar bill, as they used to say. And now that they wiped out that dumb-ass Don't Ask, Don't Tell, I can say it proudly."

"But you're...so masculine. Tough."

"So are you, in case you haven't noticed."

I never thought of myself that way. Sure, I was athletic enough to play high-school sports, and I'd made it through basic training without too much trouble. But inside I was still a shy, gay kid who didn't know what to make of his attraction to other men.

"Are you just going to sit over there?" Alec asked, breaking me out of my reverie. "Not daydreaming again, are you?"

I clambered over to sit next to him. "No need. I have a walking wet dream right here."

I leaned toward him, and he met me halfway. His lips were as dry as mine, but we managed. He opened his mouth a bit and his tongue came out, teasing its way along my lips. I opened up and our tongues met. With one arm around his shoulders,

I pulled him closer, and the passion that had been simmering inside me rose to a boiling point.

My hands roamed over his broad back, feeling his muscles beneath his T-shirt. He didn't have as much flexibility in his hands so they stayed on my shoulders, holding me close. After we'd kissed for a couple of minutes, though, I pulled back.

"What if the old guy comes back?" I asked. My heart was beating like a high-school drummer and my breathing was shallow. "We don't want these guys to know we're gay."

Alec looked up at the crack in the ceiling. "You're right. He pops in unexpectedly sometimes. But once he's delivered supper, that's the last we'll see of him until sunrise."

I backed away. "Then you can be my after-dinner treat," I said.

"Dessert," he said, smiling back at me.

The next couple of hours were hell. I kept looking up at the crack between the roof and the wall and trying to will the sun to go down faster. To distract myself from thinking of Alec naked, I focused on remembering everything I could about our surroundings.

The school building was tucked into the side of the mountain. The truck carrying me had parked a few hundred feet downhill, and I had been manhandled up a curving dirt pathway beaten into the mountainside. As we climbed, I noticed a cluster of buildings in the valley—simple houses of stone and concrete block, with corrugated metal roofs. I had no idea what the village's name was, or where we were. I had only been in Afghanistan for three months by then, and my command of the country's geography was slim.

I focused my mind on the approach to the school's front door. I had noticed that inscription above the lintel and recognized the building's original function immediately. The two men guarding me had walked me through a large classroom, though the few remaining chairs and desks had been broken into kindling and piled along one wall.

That was it. I'd been pushed into the cell with Alec directly from that room. Where had the water come from, then? And the bread? I knew there were often springs in these mountains. But the bread had to have come from the village. Did the man go down there to get it, or did someone bring it to him?

The light was almost completely gone before the door banged open again. This time the old man held a large pot in his hand which smelled of fermented goat's milk, coriander, garlic and onions. It was accompanied by two more slabs of bread—nowhere near as fresh as the ones we'd had before.

"When can this man see a doctor?" I demanded of the old man. "Is there anyone in the village who can help him?"

"I am just an old man," he said, putting the pot and the bread on the floor. "Others return in two days."

He backed out of the cell and slammed the door behind him.

I sat on the floor across from Alec and we took turns dipping bits of bread into the stew. We were both so hungry the bowl was clean in minutes.

"Two days," I said, when we were finished. "At least we have a chance to keep track of time now."

"We don't want to be here when they get back," Alec said. "If what he said is true, then right now he's the only one watching us. Tomorrow morning when he brings breakfast, I say we tackle him and get out of here."

"Where would we go? We don't even know where we are."

"I've spent a lot of time in this country. Get me outside and I'll figure it out."

"Do you think the old guy sleeps here?" I asked.

He shook his head. "He goes down to the village. But there's no way out of here. Believe me, I've tried."

"That wasn't what I was thinking of."

He looked at me. There was just enough light left in the room that I could see a glimmer in his eyes. "Oh," he said.

"Yeah. Oh." I scooted over next to him. "We need to get some sleep if we're going to break out of here tomorrow. But it's going to be a long time until dawn. You think we could…"

His mouth was on mine before I could finish the sentence. We kissed with a wild passion, pressing our faces together as if we could merge into one being. I reached down and pulled up the tails of his T-shirt, and he backed away from me long enough to get it off. I did the same thing with my own, unbuckling my pants with frenzied fingers.

It was cooling in the cell, but I was so desperate to get naked I didn't care. I had to struggle with my boots; Alec had a head start because I'd already removed one of his earlier. So he was naked first and launched himself at me while my pants were clustered around one ankle.

We couldn't wait. His mouth was on my nipple, and I arched my head back in ecstasy, running my fingers through his short hair. I reached down to find one of his nipples with my fingers, and he squirmed as I squeezed hard with my nails.

I pulled back and wriggled around beneath him. "Watch your ankle," I said.

"Fuck my ankle."

"I'd rather fuck your mouth," I said, positioning myself so we were both dick to lips. I took in as much of his as I could, but he was long and thick and I started to choke almost immediately.

He did a better job with me, and I began to mimic his actions. Licking his dick up and down like a lollypop, then teasing the head with my tongue, only taking him in my mouth when I felt good and ready.

He started humping his ass up and down, pushing into my mouth farther and farther, and then he erupted down my throat. I tried to swallow but ended up choking again. He pulled back. "Are you all right?"

"Don't stop," I pleaded, between coughs. "Jesus, don't stop."

He went down on me again, and stuck a finger roughly up my ass, and my gonads exploded. He was a better man than I was; he swallowed every drop.

Then he slumped down next to me on his right side. "That was crazy," he said.

"My first time," I said.

"No shit?"

"Well, my first time with a fellow soldier on a dirt floor in a holding cell," I said.

He flicked his index finger at my softening dick.

I pulled back. "Ow!"

He laughed. "We'd better get some sleep," he said.

"It's getting cold in here. Do you cuddle?"

He looked at me, and laughed. "Hell, yes," he said. "Scoot around."

I turned so that my head was beside his, and shifted to one side. He put his arm around me and pulled me close, his dick rested against the firm globes of my ass. I draped our clothes over our naked bodies. Then he was asleep, and so was I.

The sound of him pissing in the bucket in the corner woke me a couple of hours later. "Sorry," he said.

I stood up next to him and aimed at the bucket. There was something weirdly erotic about being naked beside him, our streams merging. "As long as we're awake, we should work out a plan," he said.

"I was thinking. When the old man put the food down on the floor last night, I had a clear shot at his neck. I could probably knock him out."

"We need better than probably."

"I studied some karate when I was a kid," I said. "My dad thought it would toughen me up. I can do it."

"If you can get him down, we can lock him here in the cell and then get out of here," Alec said.

The temperature had dropped rapidly during the night, and it was cold. We both pulled our clothes back on, then cuddled back together. When I woke again a thin stream of weak light filtered in through the crack at the ceiling. I yawned and sat up.

"About last night," Alec said.

I looked at him. Was he going to tell me that our frenzied sex had been a big mistake? He was gorgeous, after all. He could have his pick of men, military or civilian. I was sure he didn't want to get tied up in any kind of relationship. But I tried to play it light. "You mean you had the same dream I did?"

He laughed. "I'm usually not such a bastard," he said. "And I don't usually get off so fast, or choke a guy."

So he wasn't rationalizing away the night before? "I'm tough," I said, keeping up my facade. "I can take it."

"I can see that," he said. "If we do manage to get out of here, we're going to have to rely on each other. I want you to know you can count on me. That I'm not some selfish dipshit."

"You weren't selfish last night," I said. If he was going to be honest, so was I. "You were hot and sexy and those few minutes were some of the best I've ever had."

"I don't know if I should be flattered, or sad for you."

"Be flattered. I've had good sex and bad sex and great sex, and I know the difference. Last night was great."

"It was pretty hot," he admitted. "I didn't screw around

much in college, and after I got into the Army the only chances I had were on R&R, and most of the guys I met didn't really do it for me. But there's something about you—or you and me together." He looked down at the dirt floor. "I don't know how to explain it."

He didn't get a chance to, because the door swung open and the old man stepped in, carrying more fresh bread. When his head was bowed in front of me, I clasped my hands together and slammed them against his neck. He fell to the ground and Alec scrambled to his feet. I heard him wince once as he must have landed on his bad ankle, but that was it.

I pushed the man to the side and picked up the bread he had been carrying. Alec stood at the doorway to our cell and looked out. "Looks clear," he said, and stepped into the schoolroom. I was right behind him, stopping to close and lock the cell door behind me.

The room was as I remembered it—dirt floor, boarded-up windows, a pile of broken furniture in the corner. Early-morning daylight sifted in through the front door, which the old man had left ajar.

Alec grabbed a long piece of wood that looked like it had been the leg of a desk and used it as a crutch. I picked up another piece with a sharpened edge. We paused again at the front door. A rosy dawn was rising over the valley. Smoke from what I thought was a communal oven in the village lifted skyward in a thin plume. I couldn't see anyone moving there.

I closed the door behind me and we started down the winding path, Alec in the lead. We gobbled the bread as we walked. He was using the table leg as a makeshift cane, but he was able to move fast enough that I had to hustle to keep up with him. We went down the curving path, then cut away from the town, toward the north.

"I recognize this country," Alec said after a couple of minutes. "We're in the northeast, and the border with Tajikistan is that way."

"You think it's better to go that way than to try for one of the bases?"

"The closest is Bagram, outside Kabul. Long way to go, though, and it's on the other side of those mountains." He pointed south. "The countryside between here and the Tajik border is flatter and as long as we run parallel to that road down there, but out of sight, we should be able to make it in three days' march."

"Can you walk that far?"

"Going to have to."

We trudged along all morning, making our way through a rift in the mountains. We saw no one and heard nothing more than the sound of the wind rolling through the mountains. I spotted the extravagantly twisted horns of a wild goat across a valley from us, its brown body blending with the landscape as it scrambled up the rocky slope.

"That's an ibex, isn't it?" I asked, pointing. "Look at that long beard."

Alec shook his head "That's a markhor. They both have beards, but the horns of the ibex curve up like a crescent moon. The markhor's look more like a unicorn's horn."

"I wouldn't want to meet either of them up here."

"They're not the ones to worry about. There are nine species of wildcats in these mountains," Alec said. "But they're all nocturnal hunters, so with luck, we won't run across any of them. Snow leopards and black bears, too."

Alec and I took off our jackets and tied them around our waists when the sun got hot. A couple of eagles soared on the thermals above us. My throat began to parch, and I wished we'd been able to provision ourselves before our escape.

Alec stopped. "Listen."

All I heard was the wind creeping around the base of the mountain.

"Sounds like water," he said. "Over that way."

He picked up the pace, climbing around a rock formation. Below us we saw a small mountain lake surrounded by trees. A falcon that had been drinking from the water's edge rose up as we picked our way through the rocky scree. As we moved out of our cover and into the open we both scanned the area around us, but we were alone.

When we got close, I realized that the trees around the lake were a mix of olive, apricot and pomegranates. Alec lowered himself carefully to the ground, and leaned down to the lake to drink. I kept watch while he did, grabbing one of the red low-hanging globes. The apricots were tiny and unripe, but the pomegranates looked as good as any in a U.S. grocery.

When Alec sat up, I leaned down to drink myself. The water was cool and fresh and went a long way toward slaking my thirst. "You know your way around out here," I said, wiping the water from my mouth.

"Had to. Memorized the maps and potable water for most of the area."

The sun was directly overhead by then, and the basin around the lake was steaming hot. "Let's take cover in the shade," he said. "Give the heat a chance to burn off. Then we'll head out again when it cools down."

"Sounds good to me." I stood up and pulled down a couple more pomegranates, tossing them to Alec on the ground. Then I pulled the file out of my shoe and sliced into the dark red skin, letting the juice dribble into my mouth as I gobbled the ruby-colored seeds. I handed the file to Alec and he did the same.

We devoured the fruit until we were full and covered with berry stains. "Think it's safe to clean up in the lake?" I asked.

He looked around. "Can't hear anyone out there. And no one lives anywhere around this area."

"That's all I needed to hear," I said. I pulled off my red-stained T-shirt, exposing my sweaty flesh to the sun. When I looked at Alec he was staring at me.

"What?"

"You look even better in the daylight."

"Yeah, well, how's about reciprocating?" I said, as I leaned down to tug off my boots. When I looked up again, Alec had shed his boots and his T-shirt and was unbuttoning his pants. His chest was a wonder, his pecs big and beefy, his six-pack glistening with a sheen of sweat. As he shagged his pants down I got a tantalizing view of his waist, the way his lower ribs curved inward, his belly button flecked with a couple of blond hairs.

He was gorgeous, a beefy David come to life in Army-issued boxers. He peeled the bandages off his hands and looked at them. "Not bad," he said. "Healing."

I scrambled out of my pants and boxers, my dick already stiff and banging up against my belly. He turned before I could get a good view of his dick in daylight, showing me the plump globes of his ass, a few shades paler than the rest of his body. He waded gingerly into the lake, and when he got waist deep he dove under the surface.

I followed him in. The lake water was cool but not cold, warmed by the hot sun. He popped up beside me, shaking water from his smooth skin like a happy puppy dog. He pushed me backward, and I went into the water, and then the two of us were frolicking around together. We swam apart, then together, each trying to dunk the other.

For a couple of minutes we forgot that we were escaped

prisoners in the middle of a war zone. We were just two horny naked guys playing around in a sparkling mountain lake.

But all good things must end. After a half hour or so of play, I returned to shore, grabbed Alec's T-shirt and boxers and my own, and rinsed them out in the water, then lay them out in the sun to dry.

I relaxed in the shallow water by the shore, my body half-submerged, and Alec stood up and began walking toward me. His dick was everything I remembered it to be and more. It was long and firm, with a thick mushroom head.

I stood up in front of him. He had about two inches in height on me, but that didn't make a difference; he just spread his legs a little wider and we were at the same level. He wrapped his rough hands around me, playing with the fine dusting of dark hair over my ass. "I like a hairy guy," he said into my neck.

"And I like my men smooth," I said. "Seems like we're a good match."

"In more ways than one," he said.

He clasped me close to him, and we began rubbing our bodies against each other. Our dicks stiffened, the sheen of water between us acting as a lubricant. We pressed our lips together, kissing with the same wild passion we'd felt back in the cell. We struggled for maximum skin-to-skin contact, dicks rubbing against bellies. The pain-to-pleasure ratio was so equal—I wanted to pull away to relieve the tension but I couldn't let go of him, and it seemed he felt the same way.

My guts boiled and shivers raced through my body as my orgasm built and then exploded. Alec held me even closer, pressing his body against mine, his dick some kind of desperate force pushing against me, and my orgasm spiraled to heights I'd never reached before. He threw his head back and gasped and then I felt him spurt against me.

I couldn't let him go. I held him close, neither of us moving for a moment as we sagged together, relishing the force of our orgasms. Then we dunked, together, rinsing ourselves clean once more. We stood in the sun for a couple of minutes letting the air dry us off.

Alec took the first watch while I napped in the shade. He woke me after an hour then catnapped himself. The sun began to sink in the west and the air cooled down enough so that soon we would be able to walk again without risk of heatstroke. He was so handsome as he slept, the fierceness of his features relaxed, and I could see in his face the little boy he had once been.

I assumed we'd make it out of the mountains alive. Alec was strong and resourceful, and I was a good soldier. But what would happen after that? I would return to my battalion, and he'd go back to whatever it was he did. Would we ever see each other again?

I remembered my fantasy of walking away from the war. Could Alec and I do that? Slip into Tajikistan, live together under the radar in some village?

Nope. Alec wasn't the type to run away, and I realized I wasn't either. I wanted to complete my tour, do the best I could to help this parched, angry country and its people. Once my obligations were complete, I could consider what the future held. If Alec wanted to be a part of that...

He opened his eyes and smiled at me. Then he sat up, yawned and stretched. "Let's get on the road," he said.

We didn't have to go far. We climbed back up to the ridge and marched for about an hour, until Alec's eagle eye made out a U.S. recon patrol on the road below us—two big Humvees. We scrambled down the hillside in time to flag it down.

There wasn't room for both of us in either vehicle, so we

were separated. After I explained who I was and what I was doing out there, I discovered they were heading to Bagram, and leaned back in my seat and slept. It was late at night when we finally arrived at the base. Both of us had to report in, so there wasn't much time to talk.

Alec thrust a piece of paper at me and leaned close. "My email address. Next time we get together I'm thinking about spending lots of time in a king-sized bed. Sound good to you?"

"Sounds very good," I said. The Army's gotten more tolerant, but not enough that I could do what I wanted to Alec right there. Instead I reached out to shake his hand.

He grabbed me in a bear hug. "I'll see you again," he said into my ear. "Count on it."

"I'll hold you to that," I said. And then we separated to return to our assignments.

NEW DOG, OLD TRICKS

Aaron Michaels

One mile into the run, the pack felt like a lead weight on Gideon's back. After two miles, he felt like he'd strapped one of those ridiculous little Smart cars onto his shoulders. His entire upper body ached with the strain of carrying the heavy backpack, and he was sucking wind like he hadn't done since he first decided to go out for track in high school.

The day was scorchingly hot, the sun high overhead in a cloudless sky, and he was pouring sweat inside the combat camo shirt he'd picked up at the Army surplus store along with the backpack. Not the smartest time to take a run, but Gideon kept telling himself it wasn't as hot on the track as it would be in Afghanistan. It had been his stupid idea in the first place to enlist in the Army at age twenty-six, and he damn well wasn't going to Military Entrance Processing Station with a bunch of kids right out of high school without getting his body into better shape.

A few high-school kids were running on the track with

him. Or rather, passing him by, all long, sleek muscles beneath lightweight running shorts and tank tops designed to let skin breathe. At least none of them made fun of him as they zoomed past. One kid, a tall black boy who had the grace of a natural athlete, even ran next to Gideon for a few strides before he said, "*Semper Fi,*" and resumed his faster pace.

Gideon appreciated the sentiment, even if his chosen branch of the service was the Army, not the Marines.

He decided to stick it out for five miles then take a break. Technically, he was within weight range for his height. He had no medical issues that would get him disqualified, temporarily or otherwise. He didn't need to be out here for any other reason than his own pride, but that was enough to keep his feet pounding the track.

He was into mile four when another runner came up beside him. Gideon was running in the outside lane, taking his time. Most of the other runners on the track were using the inside lanes, but this guy paced alongside Gideon in the lane right next to his.

Gideon snuck a glance at the guy. Crew cut, muscular build, but not body-builder muscular, he was just little taller than Gideon and maybe about five years older. He was wearing a plain white T-shirt and running shorts and well-worn running shoes. He'd worked up a sweat, and the dog tags he wore around his neck were plainly visible through the damp, sheer fabric of his shirt.

"What company are you with, soldier?" the guy asked Gideon.

He wasn't looking at Gideon, just staring at the track ahead.

"Haven't been assigned yet, sir," Gideon said, trying hard not to sound out of breath.

The guy glanced at Gideon, one eyebrow raised. "Huh," he said, then he went back to looking at the track.

Gideon expected the guy to go back to his own run and leave Gideon behind, but the guy kept pacing him.

"When do you report?" he asked, after they'd rounded the far end of the track.

His voice sounded annoyingly normal. Gideon was staring hard at the finish line a half lap away. That was his goal. Once he crossed the finish line this time, that would mark five miles, and he could quit running and shuck the damn pack off his back.

"Two weeks," Gideon said. He didn't bother to try to mask how out of breath he was.

The guy nodded. "That ought to give you just about enough time to recover."

Gideon didn't say anything. None of the high-school kids out running had given him shit. He didn't need to take any from some soldier he didn't know. He would have pulled away and left the guy in the dust if he'd had any oomph left in his legs.

His legs felt like rubber when he crossed the finish line. The lawn in the center of the track was lush and green, and Gideon collapsed on it in an undignified heap when he tried to sit down. He slipped out of the backpack's shoulder straps and swung the thing around next to him. He had two liters of water inside along with enough dumbbell weights to equal fifty pounds. His goal was seventy pounds, but he knew enough to take that slow. He hadn't been lifting anything heavy on a regular basis since his last warehouse job went south.

He had one liter of water nearly empty when the soldier walked over to where Gideon sat. "I wasn't trying to be a smart-ass," he said. "Basic's going to be hard enough. You don't need to go in still recovering from a last-minute attempt to pull yourself into shape." He gave Gideon an obvious once-over. "Besides, you don't look all that out of shape to me."

"Thanks," Gideon said. "I think."

The soldier stuck out his hand. "Doug Evans, private first class."

Gideon's surprise must have shown on his face. The guy looked far older than someone who'd still be a PFC.

"I enlisted late, too," the guy said with a grin.

Gideon shook his hand and introduced himself. "Where are you stationed?" he asked.

"Fort Bragg, airborne forces, currently home on leave." He plopped down on the grass next to Gideon. "Staying with my sister. She just had a kid, and she wanted to introduce him to his Uncle Doug." His grin got bigger. "I'm not much into babies, but I have to say, this kid is the ugliest baby I've ever seen. Looks too much like me." He rubbed a hand across his scalp. "Even has my hair."

Gideon laughed. Now that he wasn't running and had a chance to really look, Doug wasn't half bad up close. His short hair was dark blond tinged with red, and he had the kind of skin that freckled instead of tanned. His eyes were deeper blue than the washed-out color of the summer sky, and his voice was pleasantly deep. Doug wasn't exactly Gideon's ideal kind of guy, but it had been long enough since he'd dated anyone that he couldn't help but imagine what Doug looked like beneath his clothes.

"I guess I'm going to be getting that kind of haircut soon, too," Gideon said. While his hair wasn't exactly long, he'd never had a crew cut in his life. First time for everything.

"You get used to it. Pretty easy to take care of, at any rate, and you never have to worry about having a bad hair day."

They settled into a comfortable silence. A couple of kids were still running on the track, and at the far side of the lawn, three girls sat on a blanket, their heads close to each other, talking about whatever it was that girls talked about. Gideon had never understood women, so he supposed it was a good thing that he had no interest in them whatsoever. The day was still hot, but a little breeze had kicked up from the west, and it felt good on Gideon's sweaty skin.

"So how come you're out running today when you're on leave?" Gideon asked when Doug made no move to leave.

"Same reason as you." Doug leaned back on his elbows and squinted up at the sky. "I'm older than most of the guys in my company. They go on leave, go out drinking and picking up women and still come back in the same kind of shape they were in when they left. Me? I have to work at it."

"What, no drinking and picking up girls?" Gideon teased. "Where's the fun in that?"

Doug arched one eyebrow and glanced at Gideon. "Don't get me wrong. I can drink most of those guys under the table. As for women?" He shrugged. "Not my thing, if you get what I mean."

He kept looking at Gideon, almost like he was testing whether Gideon was going to make a big deal out of what he'd just said.

"I get exactly what you mean," Gideon said. "Women aren't my thing, either."

Doug nodded. "I thought so." He grinned again. "And before you ask, no, you're not obvious, which is good. It's just that a couple of the girls I've seen out here today would have drawn the interest of half my company, but you didn't give them a second look."

Gideon thought about what Doug had just said. "How come it's good not to be obvious? I thought—"

"That things would be hunky-dory for guys like us now? Look"—Doug rolled over on his side, his head propped up on one hand—"Yeah, the brass won't discharge us anymore for engaging in a homosexual act, but that doesn't mean you aren't going to catch the same kind of shit in the Army that you'd catch in a backwoods bar down South. People are people, in uniform or out. Drill sergeants aren't going to call you a fag—they don't call anyone a fag or queer anymore—but you still have to watch your back until people get to know you."

The demise of Don't Ask, Don't Tell was one of the reasons Gideon had decided to enlist. That, and the fact that jobs were few and hard to come by these days. A few of the younger guys who'd lost their jobs along with Gideon when the warehouse went belly-up had already enlisted.

"That change your mind about enlisting?" Doug asked.

"No. I mean, I guess I was naïve to think things were different now. Back when my buddies were enlisting right out of high school, I didn't even think about it. I couldn't imagine serving an entire tour pretending to be something I wasn't."

"It was tough."

Gideon blinked. "I thought you said you were older when you enlisted?"

"I was, but I still went in when the Army was only pretending not to care I was queer. They didn't ask, I didn't tell, and I kept my dick to myself when I went out with the other guys in my company and they were hitting on anything in a skirt." He shrugged. "Danced a few times with a few pretty girls just to avoid a lot of questions, and got used to the feel of my own hand."

"So what's it like now? Do you date?"

"Nope. Not while I'm on base."

Gideon understood what Doug was telling him, and for a moment, the immediate future looked grim. Sure, Gideon didn't date much himself, but the idea of not fucking anyone at all for the next two years? Bleak.

Doug leaned closer. "Of course, that doesn't mean I don't have sex, especially when I'm on leave." His eyes traveled down Gideon's body, then back up again, slowly. "You interested?"

Gideon allowed himself a long, slow look at Doug's body in response. He had the kind of narrow hips Gideon liked, and the muscles of his legs were lean and hard, which probably meant the rest of him was muscled the same way. Gideon generally liked guys with longer hair, but he was going to have to get used to military haircuts, even on himself, and now was as good a time as any to start.

When his eyes made it back to Doug's face, he saw the man's smile had taken on a playful glint, and there was a good-humored twinkle in his eyes.

"You sure this is a good idea?" Gideon said, with a teasing smile of his own. "You do outrank me."

"You don't have a rank yet," Doug said, and he leaned in and kissed Gideon, quick and hard, on the mouth.

Gideon's legs might still feel like rubber, but his cock had no problem stiffening in response to the kiss. He was glad he'd worn track pants instead of skimpy little jogging shorts.

"I should probably take a shower," he said, when Doug backed away.

"Me, too. Plus my sister's expecting me back. How about I pick you up tonight around seven? We can go catch a movie or something first if you want."

Doug produced a cell phone from the pocket of his shorts, and he had Gideon type in his phone number and address.

When Doug got up off the grass, Gideon stood up. His back twinged in protest, and his legs felt crampy and unsteady.

"Do yourself a favor," Doug said. "Take a long, hot bath

instead of a shower. In fact, take all the baths you can before you ship off to Basic. You'll miss them. Even if you've never taken a bath before in your life, you'll miss not being able to."

He gave Gideon another quick kiss, and then he jogged off the track in the direction of the parking lot.

Seven o'clock tonight. Gideon actually had a date, and with a private first class at that. He wondered if Doug took his dog tags off when he fucked.

Gideon picked up his backpack with a groan and headed off toward the parking lot at a much slower rate. With any luck, he'd find out about the dog tags tonight.

Doug showed up at five to seven with a pizza box in one hand and a six-pack of beer in the other.

"We can still do a movie," he said, when Gideon let him into the apartment. "I just haven't had pizza like this in a while, and I had to drive right by the place on the way here."

The pizza was from a locally owned Italian restaurant that was one of Gideon's favorites. Even still in the box, it smelled delicious. His stomach rumbled. It seemed like he'd worked up a pretty good appetite with all the exercise.

"Pepperoni," Doug said, as he put the box down on the little coffee table in front of Gideon's sofa. "I figured that was a safe bet."

"Sounds great." Gideon sat down on the sofa next to Doug. "So what's the food like in the Army?"

"Not as bad as you'd think, but not as good as you'd like." Doug opened the lid of the pizza box and grabbed a slice. A long string of cheese dripped off the end. "Nothing like this, though," he said, and caught the end of the cheese with his tongue.

Gideon chuckled and grabbed for his own slice of pizza.

"I've been wondering," Doug said, after he finished off a

second slice. "Gideon's kind of an unusual name. Is there a story that goes with that?"

"Not a very interesting one. I was named after the Gideon Bible. Apparently I was conceived in a motel room on prom night." When Doug raised an eyebrow in surprise, Gideon shrugged. "There's something to be said about not over-sharing. I could never convince my mom of that."

Although, to be fair, Gideon's mom and dad had both been more than supportive when he'd told them he was gay. For a while, he'd thought they were going to be militantly supportive, but he'd finally got them to agree not to march in any gay pride parades on his behalf. He didn't want to be special because he was gay. He just wanted to be who he was, like everybody else was free to be who they were.

"I was named after General Douglas McArthur," Doug said. "My dad's greatest hero."

Something about the way he said that made it sound like a phrase he'd heard often in his life, and not under happy circumstances.

"So I guess he's happy you're in the Army then," Gideon said.

"I get a Christmas card and a birthday card from him each year, and that's it." Doug took a long drink from his beer, then put the can down on the table next to the pizza box. "He didn't react well when I told him I was gay." He turned toward Gideon and smiled. "But enough about that. Are you going to want to catch a movie? Or are we...?"

Doug let the end of the sentence trail off, but Gideon knew well enough what he meant. They were both here for sex. The food and drink and conversation had been a happy surprise, as far as Gideon was concerned.

"I think I'm good," Gideon said. "What do you have in—"

Doug didn't let him finish the sentence. He leaned in and

kissed Gideon hard, but unlike the kisses at the park, this one wasn't quick.

The man knew how to kiss, Gideon had to give him that. Doug kissed with barely banked passion, all hungry lips and thrusting tongue that Gideon sucked eagerly into his mouth. Doug's hands cupped the sides of Gideon's head, and his body pushed against Gideon until he was flat on his back on the sofa with Doug on top of him.

By the time the kiss ended, Gideon was as out of breath as he'd been at the track, and his cock was rock hard.

"Wow," Gideon said. "They teach you that in the Army?"

"I learned a lot of tricks in the Army." Doug nipped at the skin on Gideon's neck, not enough to hurt, just enough to make him shiver. "Want to see?"

"Looking forward to it."

"Okay, then." Doug got to his feet in a smooth, athletic gesture that Gideon's sore body envied. "On your feet, soldier."

It took Gideon a little more effort to get off the sofa, but he managed.

"Take that hot bath?" Doug asked.

He had. He couldn't remember the last time he'd taken a bath instead of a shower, but soaking in hot water had done wonders for his sore legs. His back was going to take a little longer before it quit being angry at him.

"Great suggestion," Gideon said. "Thanks."

"You might need another one later. I intend to teach you what being a hard-bodied Army grunt is all about."

Gideon blinked. "Are you serious?"

Doug grinned at him. "Nope. I just don't get to use lines like that too often." He took Gideon's hand and squeezed it. "Now where's your bedroom?"

Gideon had changed the sheets on his bed that afternoon

after he got out of the bath, just on the off chance that Doug wanted more action than a blow job on the sofa. He hadn't had another guy in his bed in a long time, and he'd gotten in the bad habit of washing his sheets only when he remembered, which wasn't all that often.

"Smells like fabric softener," Doug said, when he flopped on the bed to pull off his shoes. "You do that just for me?"

"Better than how it normally smells in here."

"Hey, I normally live around a bunch of sweaty, smelly guys," Doug said. "Which, by the way, doesn't hold a candle to what a poopy diaper smells like. Babies, man. I don't know why anybody would want them."

By now Doug had both his shoes off and had stripped off his shirt. His upper torso was as well muscled as his legs, with only sparse hair across his chest and a narrow treasure trail leading down past his naval. His dog tags still hung around his neck.

"Why are we talking about babies?" Gideon asked, stripping out of his own clothes.

Doug stood up and unzipped his pants, shucking them and his underwear down his legs in one fell swoop. "Because I babble when I'm nervous, and I'm always nervous when I undress in front of a guy for the first time."

From where Gideon stood, Doug had nothing to be nervous about. His belly was flat and tight, the notches of his hips looked like something out of a fashion magazine and his cock was thick and heavy and beautifully cut. He could have been a marble statue of a Greek god, had the Greeks actually let their gods be well hung. And well freckled.

"Yeah, I see why you would be," Gideon said. "You don't tan at all, do you?"

He smiled to let Doug know it was just a joke, in case Doug was sensitive about his freckles.

"Hey, rubber legs, I'm just glad I'm stationed in North Carolina these days. When I was in Afghanistan, I had a permanent sunburn."

Gideon made a mental note to ask Doug what it had been like overseas. He wanted to know, just in case that's where he ended up, but for right now he had other things on his mind.

Like finding out what Doug's cock tasted like and exactly how big his hard-on would get.

And paying Doug back for teasing him about his legs.

"Rubber legs?" Gideon arched an eyebrow.

"Better than chicken legs. Half the kids coming out of high school have these little sticks for legs. You, on the other hand..."

Doug bent over like he was going to inspect Gideon's legs up close and personal, which would have put his head level with Gideon's cock—not a bad prospect, considering Gideon's cock was at about half-mast—but then he grabbed Gideon around the waist and straightened up, and Gideon found himself bare-assed in the air over Doug's shoulder with his head hanging down Doug's bare back.

"Hey!" Gideon said, laughing in spite of his odd position. "You want to put me down?"

Doug smacked him on the ass with one hand, again not enough to hurt, just enough to send shivers through Gideon's body. "Just wanted to show you that if you're going to practice carrying around a lot of weight, there's better ways to do it."

"Okay, I get it. Can you put me down?"

This time Doug caressed his ass, his palm smooth on Gideon's skin. The shiver that coursed through Gideon's body was more pronounced this time, and he was pretty sure even Doug could feel it.

"That's one trick I learned," Doug said, as he dropped

Gideon on the bed and crawled in after him. "The smack sensitizes the skin for the caress that follows. Just like this"—Doug nipped Gideon's neck again—"sensitizes the skin for this." The soft lick with his tongue produced another shiver.

Doug pressed Gideon back against the sheets as he moved his way down Gideon's body, nipping the skin and following each gentle nip with a soft lick or kiss. When he got to Gideon's nipples, the nips were followed by sucking that shot shivers of excitement straight through to Gideon's cock.

By the time Doug had worked his way down to Gideon's navel, Gideon thought he might come before Doug even got to his cock.

"You're driving me nuts, here," he said. "I want to taste you."

"And I want to feel the inside of you," Doug said. "You got any lube?"

"Nightstand drawer. Condoms are in there, too."

While Doug reached over to grab the supplies, Gideon shifted around on the bed until Doug's cock was in his face. It looked as hard and needy as his own cock felt. He wrapped his lips around it and took it deep in his throat, and was rewarded when Doug's body shuddered in response.

"Slow down," Doug said. "I want to fuck you, not come in your mouth. That work for you?"

Gideon let the thick cock fall from his mouth. "Yeah. Oh, yeah, that definitely works for me."

He hadn't been fucked in a long time. Usually he was the one doing the fucking, but he had no objections to another guy's cock inside him. Especially when the guy knew what he was doing, which, by the way Doug was playing with his ass, was definitely the case here.

Not only was Doug finger-fucking him like a pro, he was

sucking on Gideon's balls and pressing the fingers of his other hand in just the right spot to make Gideon see stars behind his closed eyelids. Gideon couldn't help himself. He grabbed Doug's balls and started kneading, and took Doug's cock back in his mouth. He felt like he was going to come any second, and he wanted to make Doug come, too.

"God, you're a vacuum cleaner," Doug said with a groan.

He jerked his hips away from Gideon, and the next thing Gideon knew, he was on his back with his feet up in the air on Doug's shoulders. He watched as Doug rolled a condom on his own cock, still wet from Gideon's mouth.

"You ready?" Doug asked.

Gideon nodded. He was more than ready. He was so ready he felt like he might fly apart.

Doug didn't thrust in hard, but took it slow, adjusting both their bodies until Gideon arched his back and cried out. "Oh god, yes," Gideon said. "Right there."

"Hang on," Doug said, his voice tight with tension and need. "Here we go."

Doug took two more easy thrusts to let Gideon get used to his girth, and then he starting pounding away in earnest.

Gideon couldn't remember the last time he'd been fucked like that. Maybe he'd never been fucked like that. Doug kept hitting the right spot inside him over and over and over again until Gideon felt like he was nothing but sensation and need and the tight, hot feeling of an incipient orgasm that would be the best of his life if it ever got there. He realized at some point that Doug had a tight grip around the base of his balls, and he wondered if that was another trick Doug had learned in the Army.

He wanted to come so bad. He opened his eyes to look at Doug. That muscular, freckled chest was glistening with sweat, the dog tags bouncing around his neck, and Doug's face was flushed with effort, but still he kept pounding into Gideon.

"I need to come," Gideon told him. "You've got to let me come."

Doug grinned at him. "That's all you had to say." He let go of Gideon's balls and wrapped his fist around Gideon's cock.

Three solid strokes later, Gideon came. His entire body seemed to clench as he grunted his way through the most intense orgasm of his life. He was dimly aware that Doug had quit thrusting and instead had buried his cock as deep inside Gideon as he could get.

"Shit," Gideon said, once his brain started working again. "Holy shit."

"Yeah."

Gideon felt Doug slide out of him, and he dropped his legs off Doug's shoulders. He watched as Doug tied off the condom and threw it in the wastebasket next to the bed.

"That was pretty incredible," Gideon said, as Doug flopped down on the bed next to him. "I think you're right. I am going to need another bath."

"Me, too. You gave me a workout." Doug leaned over and kissed Gideon on the shoulder.

"My tub's pretty big," Gideon said. "If you want to share, that is."

"I could do that." Doug turned over on his side like he had at the track. "When did you say you're going to MEPS?"

"Two weeks." Gideon turned toward Doug. "How long's your leave?"

"Another ten days," Doug said.

Gideon trailed a finger down Doug's chest, playing connect the freckles. "Anything else you think I should know about Army life as a not-so-young, gay enlisted man?"

"Yup." Doug grinned. "A lot of stuff."

"Sounds like it might take some time to teach me."

Doug's grin got wider. "About ten days, I think. You good with that?"

"Yes, sir," Gideon said with a smile.

READY RESERVE

Logan Zachary

Every July, I returned to active duty to play solider once again for the last two weeks of the month. The reserves met, and I was back to the Army. I threw my duffle bag on the ground as I locked my Honda Civic's door and headed to the barracks.

Sweat dripped off my brow and burned my eyes as I crossed the parking lot. The first day was always difficult when the guys regrouped. Everyone talked excitedly about their children and wives. Being a single, gay man in the Army should have been better after Don't Ask, Don't Tell was repealed, but it wasn't. I was in my midforties and still unmarried, so I tended to worry about how the other guys perceived me. The confirmed bachelor seemed to be an extinct being.

The sun baked down on the asphalt, making waves of heat rise up. I doubted the barracks were air-conditioned, and if they were, the AC would suck. The units tended to give out more noise at night than cool air. If I was lucky, there would be plain fans to circulate the air.

There were always a few nights of camping and sharing a pup tent with another guy. Hopefully, the heat would break, or at least the evenings would cool off.

I opened the door and entered the blast furnace. I saluted the man with the clipboard and gave him my name: Staff Sergeant Thomas Clay reporting for duty.

I found my locker and quickly made my bed. All my gear was stowed and ready for inspection or whatever they had in store for us. Every summer it was the same and different. We were assigned a buddy to spend the two weeks with. We did everything together and shared the living space.

Sometimes we were paired with guys we knew, and sometimes, due to vacations and transfers, we met a new solider. This year I had a new partner, Sergeant Joe Harris. I hoped he wouldn't be a talker. Telling me his entire life story and expecting me to spill my guts to him. Whatever happened to loose lips sink ships? I'm sure the Navy wouldn't share their motto with us. Or showing me picture after picture of his kids, his dog, his wife, his boat, his...

I ran my hand over my new buzz cut. I had gone to the little Korean man at my neighborhood barber shop and told him to scalp me, before the service did. Twelve bucks for a haircut: very cheap for Minneapolis establishments. I always gave him a twenty. A nice tip, and he was always happy to see me.

The sun had bleached my blond to almost white, and my skin was golden brown. I worked construction all summer as I was off my regular teaching job. Three months to either fix my place up or get hired out to fix someone else's. I wished my teacher's salary was a big as a pro athlete's, but the reserves added to my net worth.

Once all was unpacked, I headed over to the mess hall and

waited for dinner. Guys milled around, and I recognized a few. I ate quickly and headed out to the night, hoping to catch a cool breeze. But the evening was dead silent, except for the frogs and the crickets that prayed for rain.

Sergeant Harris lay across his upper bunk working on the daily crossword puzzle when I came in for the night. He wore a loose-fitting T-shirt and sweats. Standing, he offered me his hand. "Nice to meet you, Thomas. I hear we're partners for the next two weeks."

His hand was warm and firm as he took mine. He shook it with power and authority, but not with pure power to show me how strong he thought he was. His hair was dark brown with a slight curl to it. Blue eyes, even white teeth and what appeared like a muscular body. He topped out at six foot even, five inches taller than me.

"Nice to meet you. You're a lot taller than I am. Would the bottom bunk work better for you?"

Harris smiled as he let go of my hand. "If you're fine with this body lying above you all night, I'm fine with it too. I'd hang over the end of the bed above or below you."

Images flashed through my mind, as I struggled to keep them in check. I yawned and pointed to the bathroom. "I'm about ready to call it a night." I moved over to my locker to get my toothbrush and paste.

"I'm almost done with my puzzle, and I was headed that way myself." He bounded back into bed with his paper and pen and watched me head to the latrine.

Our morning started with our physical training, and after our five-mile run, we headed to the mess hall for breakfast.

I ate and hurried back to the barracks to shower before our

next class started. I didn't want to be all sweaty for our CPR recertification. I had turned off the water and was starting to dry off as Sergeant Harris entered the shower room.

"I turned my back to you, and you disappeared." He tossed his towel over a hook and walked straight at me. His thick penis bounced off each leg as he walked. His low-hanging hairy sac swung easily between his long hairy legs. He looked like a model on the runway. He smiled at me and I felt my dick start to swell.

How could I be partnered with him for the next two weeks? This was going to be hell.

"I need to be clean before I can do CPR. I see you do too. I don't know how anyone can concentrate when they're sweaty and stinky." He turned on the water, and the spray cascaded over his body, making the hair darker against his tan body. A square-cut swimsuit tan line showed a white ass and pelvis. He turned to face the water and his perfectly sculpted ass dimpled as he moved. His cheeks were smooth as could be and as he bent over, a tight pink pucker winked at me.

I fumbled the towel as I dried between my legs and tried to hide my swelling penis. "Did they change the rules again this year?" My voice sounded squeaky as I asked.

"Isn't that the point? Change it each year so we have to learn it and test out of it." He looked over his shoulder. His torso twisted to reveal a lean form of rippling muscles. The bronzed skin showed each muscle to fine definition.

I wrapped the towel around me and headed back to my locker. I jumped into my boxers, still damp as I tried to pull them up over my ass. I struggled to get them up, but the elastic waistband rolled and bunched up underneath the towel.

A hand slipped into my underwear and brushed my hairy butt. The fingers rolled the material flat and smoothed it out, before pulling it up in back. He patted my bottom and moved over to his locker.

"My kids always get stuck in their clothes." Harris dried his back with his towel, still flashing his amazing backside at me. With each step, the glutes flexed and dimpled.

"I guess I haven't grown up yet either." I pulled the damp towel from around my waist and ran it over my dripping head.

Harris bent over into his locker and pulled out a pair of boxers. He stepped into them, making his white cheeks disappear.

My heart seemed to sigh in my chest. "I'm wearing shorts and a T-shirt. I hear the AC is out and the classroom is in direct sun."

"Crap. Why do we have training in the summer? Can't we get a cold month for a change? I hate losing two weeks of my summer. My kids complain, and they want to come with me."

"They love to camp?" I asked as I pulled my T-shirt over my head.

"They would rather be here than me. Give me the mower and a cold beer." He pulled on a pair of baggy shorts over his boxers. He found a sleeveless shirt with large openings on each side of it. His naked torso was framed in the cotton.

I bit my lower lip as I found my shorts and socks.

He sat on his bunk to pull on his socks and I noted his long, hairy toes. As he sat, his shorts leg peeked open and revealed a hairy testicle dangling along one of his legs.

I bit down harder. How the fuck was I going to be able to concentrate now?

"Did they give you a Red Cross CPR book?" Harris uncrossed his legs and switched feet.

I tried not to look, but I couldn't help it. I was weak. His thick cock dangled down his other pant leg.

Double damn.

I knew my shorts would be pitching a tent sooner than we needed one.

Harris knelt on the floor over the mannequin as he started CPR. His shorts hugged his ass, deep into the crease and tight over his muscular buttocks. The waistband slipped down a bit to show a triangle of hair in the small of his back.

I wanted to comb my fingers through that patch of hair so badly. I dropped the CPR booklet and lost my page.

"How many compressions am I supposed to do?" Harris looked up at me, expecting an answer.

I flipped through the book, trying to find the page.

Harris rose up and I noticed his shorts had ridden up and a pink, hairy orb peeked out of a leg as he reached across the mannequin. A white band of skin contrasted from his tan as his shorts and shirt parted.

"Get down here and help me," he demanded.

I moved to the opposite side of the mannequin. I looked into his deep blue eyes and smiled. "I don't have a clue where it is."

He reached over and grabbed the book from my hand and then sat back on his feet. His shorts were pulled tight over his groin and outlined his package. One testicle had slipped down and the rounded furry tip peeked out.

He arched his back and thrust his pelvis even farther into my line of view.

Was he doing that on purpose? Was he coming on to me?

"It's your turn to pump and blow, pump and blow. I want to see your technique."

What did he mean by that? I swallowed hard and started CPR.

* * *

Next day, we had our orders and headed out to camp for three days: setting up, building a latrine and cooking our own food, as we played war games and worked on strategies of warfare.

I crawled into our tent and settled into my sleeping bag. The night was hot and humid and not a breeze blew in the evening sky. I usually slept naked at home, but since I had to share quarters, I kept on a pair of boxers and a T-shirt.

Sergeant Harris unzipped the tent and entered. He smelled of Crest toothpaste and a shower with Irish Spring. I inhaled deeply and stopped suddenly. I worried he would hear me and figure out what I was doing.

"Hot one tonight." Harris unbuttoned his shirt and pulled it off one shoulder and then the other. He wore a wifebeater underneath and pulled that off too. His muscles rippled underneath his bronze skin. A reddish tinge from the sun covered his chest and back.

"It's only for two days." I rolled over onto my side to watch him undress.

He unbuckled his belt and unzipped his fly. His hairy belly filtered down into his boxers waistband. His fly winked open to reveal thick, curly hair inside.

I lay back down and stared at the peak of the tent. A spot in the canvas held my attention as Harris struggled in the cramped space to get his pants off.

He sat down and brought his legs up, pulling his pants off the rest of the way. He kicked his hairy legs, making his muscles stand out as he stretched. His feet sprang free, and he flopped down on his back onto his sleeping bag. He let his legs drop, allowing them to spread wide, and one foot landed on my sleeping bag. His toe brushed against my leg.

My leg felt as if it burned from his touch. Instinct almost

made me pull it away, but desire forced me to keep it there. The
air in the tent was hot and humid. A sheen of sweat covered my
body. The night had done little to cool the heat of the day away.

"Man, I'm beat. What a day. I'm sure the heat and humidity
are kicking my butt." Harris rolled on his side to face me.

I could feel his eyes on me. Out of the corner of my eye, I
watched as he adjusted himself in his boxers. I knew I couldn't
be rude, so I rolled on my side to face him. "Camping can be
fun, but this seems like a lot of work."

"If we're ever in combat, I'm sure they want us to be able to
survive in a tent."

My sleeping bag was cooking me alive. I pulled my underwear away from my balls and out of the crack in my ass before
taking my arms out of the bag and letting them air out. "At least
it's only for a few nights."

"How can you stay in that bag? I'd burst into flames. You
should at least take off your T-shirt." He motioned for me to
follow his orders.

I reached into the sleeping bag and pulled my shirt off and
over my head. I placed it above my pillow.

Harris reached over, picked it up and brought it to his face.
He inhaled. "You're soaking wet." He twisted his body as he
tossed my shirt back. His boxers slipped down his hip and
showed the crest of his butt. The furry patch in the small of his
back trailed lower and into his crease. When he looked at me,
he noticed my gaze. He rolled over onto his belly and pushed
his butt up as he settled down. "This isn't the most comfortable
sleeping." He spread his legs wider to expose as much of his
body to catch a breeze if it came.

None did.

"Did you want the light on? I'm sure that's adding to the
heat."

And so are you, I thought, but just shook my head. "You can turn it off."

He reached for it, and his boxers pulled down lower on his torso, the quarter top of his ass coming into view just as the light went out, his deep hairy crack disappearing in the dark.

I didn't sleep at all that night.

My dick was raw and my boxers were soaked as I struggled out of my sleeping bag. I unzipped the entire bag to let it dry out during the day.

I crawled out of the tent, and Harris was on my tail. I wrapped my towel around my body and headed to the latrine. Harris followed close behind, and as we finished our morning pee, he cocked his head to the side and said, "There's a pond over there where we could wash before starting the day." His boxers stuck to him like a second skin. "I'm sticky and need a dip. Going to join me?" He headed off without waiting for a reply.

I followed, watching his butt bounce and sway from side to side and up and down.

Harris took off running and dove into the pond from a wooden dock that led out onto clear fresh water. I followed and looked into the water as he splashed around.

"Come in, it's warm."

I stepped off the dock and entered cold water. My head disappeared under the surface as every nerve ending screamed with cold and refreshment. Bubbles flowed over my body and up my boxers as I floated up to the surface.

I spat out the water and opened my eyes. "Wow, that woke me up."

"Good," Harris said, and smiled. He dove under the water

and swam to me. He slowly rose in front of me. His blue eyes sparkled in the morning sun. He touched my shoulder and said, "I'll race you to the dock." And he took off with a splash.

Despite his longer arms and legs, I beat him. I climbed out of the water and watched as he did the same. His boxers were almost see-through and it looked like he had morning wood. But if that was so, shouldn't the major timber have gone down after we peed?

I looked down and realized I mirrored him.

Harris smirked and walked down the wooden planks to get his towel. He picked up mine and handed it to me. His hand brushed mine for a few seconds, and he held it there. Goose bumps rose over me and not from the water's chill.

"Let's go get breakfast," he said.

I walked behind him and enjoyed the view. It looked like he wore nothing. The illusion was only ruined by his elastic waistband.

The rest of the day was spent playing war games, challenging our shooting skills and tactical skills, and seeing how well we could read a map and use the compass and sights for possible aerial attacks.

The heat of the day beat down on us and I drank as much water as I could to stay hydrated. Two men passed out and had to be sent to the infirmary for IV fluids to rehydrate them.

Harris motioned for me after supper to head over to the latrine. "Let's go skinny-dipping. It'll cool us off before bed."

I dreaded to see how hot our tent was going to be and this was the only way to really cool off. "Lead on."

We stripped off our clothes back to back and jumped into the water, then swam for a while to relax our sore muscles. Once cool, we floated together.

"I guess it could be worse," I said.

"How?" Harris smiled as he sank lower into the water until only his eyes were above the surface.

"I've had some partners that are so intense and no fun. They couldn't relax to save their life and would never do this in a million years."

"You have to make the best out of life," Harris said. "If you don't no one else will."

What simple advice and such great insight. "I guess we do make our experiences better or worse by how we see them and react to them."

Harris moved closer to me. I could feel his body heat radiate through the water.

He kicked his legs in front of me, treaded water and looked at me.

I was instantly hard and wondered if he could see, and then I wanted to see if he was too, but couldn't look down. His gaze held mine.

He moved closer.

We could almost touch and my body tensed. I felt he was going to kiss me, but he held his distance and floated.

My breathing increased, and my whole body tingled with a schoolgirl crush. What was he doing to me? He was married with children. Was he flirting? What the hell was going on?

His leg brushed against mine in the water. "Should we head back?" His voice was so smooth and calm.

"Sure," I shivered. Not sure whether it was from the cold water or the heat I felt for Harris.

We climbed out of the water, and I used my undershirt to dry off.

Harris shook his body like a dog, spraying water everywhere. His hair tightened into smaller curls when wet.

We dressed in silence and headed back to our tent. Stopping at the latrine to empty our bladders was the last event before crawling into the inferno.

I pulled my damp clothes off and spread them out. As I started to slip into my sleeping bag, Harris turned to me and said, "Are you sure you want to get in there? You'll cook inside and never get any sleep."

"I didn't sleep well last night, but after today, I should." I pushed the top of the sleeping bag back and lay on the inside.

Harris stripped down to his shorts and lay on top of his bag. He brought his hands behind his head and sighed.

I looked at the hair in his armpit and across his chest. My gaze traveled lower and noticed a bulge in his boxers. The fly gaped open, and dark hair sprouted out of the hole.

"It must be hard," Harris said.

"What?" Had he caught me looking? Was I daydreaming and I missed something? I looked at him startled.

His easy smile calmed me. He rolled onto his side and rested his head on his palm. He looked up and down my body before he spoke. He reached over and touched my shoulder. He drew his finger over my collarbone and to the base of my neck. He paused for a second and headed south between my pecs. He combed the hair into a part, lower and lower.

I closed my eyes as he stopped at the bottom of my pecs, but he continued lower, across my abs, over one bump, to the next to the next. He paused above my belly button and followed the hair around and around. He dipped into it and tickled me, but I held perfectly still.

He popped out of the navel and continued down.

He approached my waistband where the hair thickened. *Touch it, touch it, touch it.*

He traced my waistband and ran his finger back and forth.

Each pass, he pressed deeper into my torso, inching underneath the waistband, lower.

I stopped breathing. My body tensed and trembled as he traced deeper. My dick had been down in my boxers, but now it arced.

"Relax," he whispered. His fingertip touched the base of my dick.

It leapt in my boxers and pulled up. It slapped the back of his hand and bounced off of it.

His hand flipped, and his fingers wrapped around my shaft. He held me in his grasp. Ever so slowly, he stroked up and down barely a millimeter. Up and down, he stroked and my cock swelled in his hand.

"Beautiful," was all he said, as he rose up onto his knees.

"I..." I started to speak, but he reached over with his other hand and placed a finger over my lips.

"Shhh." He brought his lips down to mine and hovered over them. They opened as mine parted and we kissed. Long, deep and slow, his tongue touching mine. He straddled my body so that we were pelvis to pelvis. His erection rubbed along mine.

I pressed up against him and wrapped my arms around his neck, pulling his face down to my mouth. Deeper his tongue entered. He knew how to kiss. My hands released his neck and followed down his body. My fingers found his underwear and pushed them down.

His butt bared but his thick cock held his shorts in place.

I switched to the front of his boxers and pulled harder, releasing his dick. It swung free as he pulled mine off.

He set his naked body on mine and electricity flowed over us. Each nerve in me desired more. He humped me and his cock slid along mine. Precome oozed out of me and made our dicks slide against each other more easily. His hairy balls tickled mine as he pumped back and forth.

I grabbed and squeezed his buttcheeks and kneaded the solid muscles. I pulled them apart and let my fingers trace along his crease. He moaned with pleasure as I explored. He moved lower and his hard-on slipped between my legs and probed.

I arched my back and allowed easier access. His thick shaft stretched me as it sought deeper entry to my opening. I pulled harder on his ass, driving him on to me, wanting him deep inside me.

He reached over to his bag and pulled out a bottle of lube. I didn't even question why a straight man would have a bottle. He pulled out a condom and set it next to us. He spread lube along his dick and applied a healthy coating to my butt. His finger found my hole and worked lube inside. He circled and pressed in only to circle again. His thick finger spread my tender opening.

"You're tight," he said.

"Ahh," was all I could say.

He applied another coating to his cock and returned to try two fingers in me. Inch by inch, he entered, slowly stretching me and making me beg for more. His other hand found my dick and he slicked it up and down. The added sensation relaxed me more, and my legs spread wider.

His heavy balls swung back and forth as he pushed himself between my legs and positioned his condom-coated cock to me. Back and forth he rocked as he stroked my cock.

My hole opened and swallowed him slowly.

"I'm going to shoot," he said in a panicked voice.

I held perfectly still and allowed him to calm his overly excited flesh.

He worked my cock as he remained buried deep inside me. Faster and faster, he stroked me; he thrust his penis into me as his hand rolled over my fat mushroom head. He pounded on my prostate as he jacked me off. He found his control and started to hump me faster and harder. Each thrust, he pulled out and pushed in deeper.

Precome flowed out of me and down my shaft, mixing with the lube.

His hand squeezed harder and faster.

I grabbed my legs and pulled them as wide as I could. The tension increased across my body and added to the excitement of his thrusts.

"Faster."

He doubled his pace.

"Harder."

Skin slapped skin, lube sprayed across us.

Sweat broke out over us and made the lube slide easier. I couldn't take it anymore. My body jerked as his dick hit my spot, and my dick exploded in his hand. The thick hot load filled his palm and he pulled it down my sensitive cock and caused another explosion.

He thrust hard into me one last time and emptied his balls. The heat filled me up and sent another wave out of my dick.

He humped me a few more times and milked out a few more spasms of joy. He leaned forward and kissed me, his mouth hungrily tasting mine. His body descended on me and slipped easily over me with all the fluids. He slowly pulled out of me and gasped as the thick head popped free.

His cock lay next to mine and throbbed. He rolled over me and came up behind me and held me spooned to his body. His hands slowly caressed my inflamed body.

I wanted to scream *Stop*, but I didn't want it to end.

He licked along my ear. "I want you in me next time." And he kissed down my neck.

All I could focus on was that there would be a next time, and I smiled as I fell asleep in his arms.

Harris and I had a fantastic week. Every activity challenged and engaged us. Any moment we could escape and enjoy each other's company was used to its full benefit. After our last class and test, it was time to pack up our duffle bags. As I folded the last of my clothes and stuffed them in, I asked him, "Do you need a ride to the airport?"

Harris turned and looked at me with a smile. "Thanks, I'd love that. I hate the Army transport. We may get through security faster, but the trip sucks."

I closed my bag and knew I was done. I watched as Harris finished his packing.

He picked up his bag and said, "Ready."

We waved at a few of the guys still there, exited the barracks and walked into the parking lot.

As Harris and I walked to my car, his cell phone rang. He opened and spoke, "Hi Honey."

I unlocked the door and flipped the locks for all the doors. I took our bags and placed them in the trunk.

"Honey, there was a slight problem with my plane ticket, and I won't be flying home tonight." He looked over at me.

I met his gaze. "Honey?" I mouthed.

"Yeah, they're putting me up in a Jacuzzi suite, with a fireplace and champagne and all the room service I could want. A perfect view of the city and ice-cold air conditioning."

Did he mean what I thought he was saying?

"Okay, kiss the kids, and I'll see you late tomorrow night." He closed his phone and opened the door. "Are you ready to head to the hotel?"

"Didn't you have a flight?"

"It's been delayed until tomorrow. I have other plans for tonight." His smile and the twinkle in his eyes told me what he wanted.

"And who is 'honey'?" I asked, hoping the concern didn't shade my words.

"She's my little sister, who's sitting with my kids."

"Won't she be angry having to sit for another day?"

"She won't mind, when she hears why I was delayed. She's been hoping I'd find a new boyfriend." Harris stepped next to me and looked around the parking lot to make sure no one was around. "I'm sure she'll love you once she meets you." He kissed the side of my head and ran around the car.

Opening my car door, I jumped in, fastened my seat belt and sped off to the hotel.

Harris held his hand on my knee all the way there.

SOARING

Michael Bracken

As I stared in the mirror, I adjusted my tie and straightened my uniform jacket, marveling at how much the world had changed during my years in the Air Force. Less than a year earlier I could not admit, nor could anyone ask about, my sexual orientation. Less than a year earlier I could not have married Scott and kept my commission. Less than a year earlier I could not have imagined a church filled with people about to share the moment in which Scott and I vowed eternal union.

We first met at a reception hosted by the local country club in which members wined and dined with newly transferred officers, and the socially connected locals patted themselves on the back for supporting the troops. As a captain, I'd been obligated to attend and regale the attendees with heroic tales of my recent tour of duty overseas in which I'd flown several combat missions as a jet pilot but had seen far less action than the grunts on the ground. When it became obvious that I was single, I found myself fending off the attentions of several matronly women who felt certain I would be interested in their unmarried daughters.

I finally ducked into the men's room to distance myself from their attentions and have a few minutes to gather my thoughts. Even there I wasn't alone. Scott—an attractive man in his midthirties to whom I had been introduced at some point earlier in the evening—stood at the sink washing his hands. When he glanced in the mirror and saw me, he said, "I see the old biddies are circling you like a pack of wolves, trying to interest you in their homely and oft-divorced daughters. You don't stand a chance, Captain Hunter."

I saw that he wasn't wearing a ring. "How do you deal with it?"

"Some of them have been after me for years." He winked. "But I'm not interested in women."

Before I could respond, he stepped from the restroom and left me staring at the slowly closing door.

Scott had disappeared from the reception by the time I exited the men's room and once again attracted the circling pack of matrons. I survived the rest of the evening by repeatedly assuring the women that my duties kept me far too busy to become involved with anyone, but still they foisted off their daughters' names and phone numbers. I graciously tucked each business card and scrap of paper into my pocket, but discarded them all once I returned to my quarters on base because none contained the one phone number in which I was most interested.

Scott and I didn't cross paths again until several months later. By then I was flying a desk; my daily routine kept me mostly on base, and I had resigned myself to a life of solitude and self-pleasure because I had no desire to jeopardize my military career by engaging in meaningless one-night stands. I spent many evenings with my nose in a novel and, because the PX's selection of reading material didn't coincide with my taste, I had to visit an independent bookstore off base to replenish my reading material.

While I was examining the back cover of an anthology of gay mysteries another shopper sidled up to me and said, "Captain Hunter."

When I looked up I found Scott standing beside me.

"I almost didn't recognize you out of uniform."

I wore blue jeans, a loose-fitting sweatshirt, a baseball cap and Ray-Ban Aviator sunglasses. I said, "That's the intent."

He glanced at the book I was holding. "That's an interesting choice for a man who was fighting women off with a stick the last time I saw him."

I shrugged and returned the paperback to the shelf. "I like mysteries."

"Don't we all," Scott said. "The biggest might be why you're shopping here."

I knew he wouldn't have to be Sherlock Holmes to figure it out, and I was right. He suggested we visit a little coffee shop around the corner to discuss his conclusion.

He ordered a cappuccino and I ordered coffee, black. We carried our cups to a booth in the back, out of sight of anyone who might glance in the front window.

We didn't mention the obvious, instead discussing our career choices—the Air Force for me, banking for him—and how they impacted our lives. I had elected to avoid most social situations that required my appearance as half of a couple while he had a pair of female friends who would beard for him on those occasions.

"I've lived here my entire life," he said, "and I learned young that discretion is the better part of valor."

"No one knows?"

"Only a small circle of trusted friends," he said, "and you. I travel frequently and attend to my needs when I'm away."

"That's a lonely way to live."

"You can get used to anything if you must."

"Even celibacy," I said.

"That bad?"

"It isn't anything I can't handle on my own," I said.

Scott laughed and reached across the table to touch my forearm. "Maybe someday we can find a solution to both our problems."

"Maybe," I agreed, but we didn't pursue the idea right then. We finished our coffee, exchanged contact information and parted company.

Scott was first to pick up the phone when he called a few weeks later to tell me about an upcoming trip to Dallas. "Ever been?"

I admitted that I hadn't.

"Join me," he said. "I'll show you around."

Scott drove from Enid and I hitched a ride in a transport plane from Vance Air Force Base, arriving a few hours after he did. I met him at a hotel where he had reserved a suite, and he took me to dinner, to the symphony, and then back to the suite where a bottle of champagne chilled in an ice bucket.

"If I didn't know better," I said, as I settled onto the couch, "I'd think you were trying to seduce me."

Scott freed the champagne bottle from the bucket, uncorked it and filled a pair of glasses. He handed one to me and raised his in silent toast. As we sipped our champagne, he asked, "Is it working?"

"Quite well," I told him. After setting my half-empty glass on the coffee table, I reached for Scott's free hand and pulled him down on the couch beside me.

I hooked my hand behind his head, pulled his face close and covered his lips with mine. Our first kiss was tentative and lasted only a fraction of a second. We drew a few inches apart, stared for a moment into each other's eyes as if searching for the answer to a question neither of us dared ask and then we kissed again—deeper, harder, longer.

Scott tried to set his champagne glass on the table with mine, but he missed and it fell to the floor. He unthreaded my tie and slipped it out of my collar. Then our fingers found buttons, buckles and zippers, and we stripped off the suits we had worn to the symphony.

Scott kissed his way down my chest, paused for a moment to tease one of my nipples and then continued until he reached the base of my erection. Using just the tip of his tongue, he drew a wet line along the underside of my shaft until he reached the tip of the swollen purple head. He licked away a glistening drop of precum before taking the first few inches of my cock into his mouth.

He wrapped one fist around my stiff shaft and pistoned his hand up and down as he hoovered my hard-on. Too much time had passed since I had last been with a man and I couldn't restrain myself. Without warning, I came, firing a thick wad of hot spunk against the back of his throat.

He swallowed and swallowed again, releasing his oral grip on me while my cock was still throbbing. He slipped off the couch, stood and took my hand.

Then he led me into the bedroom, where we spent the next few hours exploring each other's bodies.

The following morning we walked through Oak Lawn, a Dallas neighborhood where no one gave us a second glance when Scott took my hand. We shopped, had lunch and shopped more. After dinner, we went club hopping, visiting three different nightclubs before we found one with the right mix of atmosphere and music to entice us onto the dance floor.

We stayed out until well past midnight and returned to our hotel suite hot, sweaty and borderline drunk. Once the door closed behind us, I pushed Scott against the door and covered his lips with mine. I shoved my tongue into his mouth and we kissed hard and deep and long, and by the time the kiss ended I'm certain he felt my erection prodding his thigh much as I felt his prodding mine.

As we kissed again, I unbuckled his belt, unsnapped his jeans and drew down his zipper. I wanted Scott and I didn't want to wait. I spun him around and tugged his jeans and briefs down to his thighs.

He pushed me backward as he grabbed them before they could drop to the floor. I reached for Scott but he spun out of my grasp and headed toward the bedroom. I followed.

He kicked off his shoes as he went, peeled off his jeans and briefs and came to a stop on his side of the bed. He grabbed the partially used tube of lube we'd used the night before and pressed it into my hand.

I squeezed a glob onto my fingers and massaged it into his asscrack and then into his asshole as he bent over the bed. I unfastened my own jeans and let them drop to my ankles. Then I pressed the swollen head of my erect cock along the lube-slicked crack of his ass until it pressed against the tight pucker of his sphincter.

As Scott pressed backward, I pushed forward, driving my cock deep into him. I held one hip with my left hand. My right hand was still covered with lube so I reached around to grasp his erect cock, and I stroked it as I drew back and pushed forward.

We'd made love our first night together. Our second night,

though, fueled in part by alcohol and in part by an entire day spent flirting with each other in public places where consummation of our desire might be frowned upon, we fucked and fucked hard.

I slammed into him again and again as I beat him off and Scott came first, spewing cum over the bed and over my fist. I released my grip on his cock and grabbed hold of his hips with both hands. I held on tight as I drove into him several more times.

Even if I had wanted to, I couldn't have held back, and I came hard, firing hot spunk deep inside my new lover. I held him tight against me until my cock finally stopped throbbing and I could withdraw.

We stripped off the rest of our clothes and fell into bed together. I wanted to take him a second time, but the long day and the alcohol had other plans for our bodies and we fell asleep in each other's arms.

Room service woke us when they brought breakfast Sunday morning, and I barely had time to eat after I showered and dressed. Then I shoved the last of my things in my ditty bag and grabbed my suit bag.

Scott caught me before I reached the door. He kissed me long and hard, and when the kiss ended, said, "Stay."

"I can't," I told him. "I have to return to base."

"I'll be here through the middle of the week," he said.

"You'll be in meetings all day."

"But I could devote my evenings to you," he said. "You have enjoyed the evenings, haven't you?"

"I appreciate your desire," I said, "but I have to leave."

"Can we talk when I return home?"

"There's nothing to talk about," I said. "As much as you want me and as much as I want you, we live in the same community and we can't spend time together there."

"I'll be discreet."

I pressed a finger against his lips. "You say that now, but what will you say later? What will you say when we meet each other on the street? What will you say when you accidentally reveal my secret? I have a lot to lose, Scott. What do you have to lose?"

He didn't answer, so I opened the door and left him standing in the hotel suite.

I hitched a ride home on the same cargo plane that had brought me, and didn't sleep well the next few nights. I'd had my share of one-night stands and short-term relationships when I was younger, but somehow Scott had gotten under my skin in a way that no previous lover ever had. But he was out, even if only to select friends and family members, where I could not be. While I might be willing to risk my heart, I wasn't willing to risk my hard-earned military career so near to retirement.

Scott called when he returned from his trip, leaving a message on my cell phone that I didn't answer, and he called again a few days later. I was able to avoid him for nearly a month by not responding to his calls and not leaving the base, but a return visit to the country club at the insistence of my commanding officer threw us together again.

"Captain Hunter," Scott said, as he thrust his hand out to clasp mine. "It's so nice to see you again. I'm surprised you were able to get away from base."

I melted inside. "I've been busy," I said, "but it looks like I'll have free time this weekend."

Before we could say any more, we were interrupted by one of the matronly women I'd met during my previous visit to the country club. This time she'd brought her daughter and she insisted on introducing us.

Scott flashed me a wicked little grin and left me to fend for myself. When I phoned later that evening, he asked if the woman had already set a wedding date for her daughter and me. I let Scott take his shot—I deserved it for the way I'd avoided him since returning from Dallas—before we began our real conversation.

We had a lot to work out, and it took more than one conversation to do it, but we soon realized we both wanted what neither of us had ever had: a relationship. And we both knew that circumstances prevented us from having a normal one. Unlike during our visit to the Oak Lawn neighborhood in Dallas, we could never hold hands in town, could never kiss in public as we had seen same-sex couples doing and could never do anything that might circumvent the purpose of Don't Ask, Don't Tell.

We were careful, almost too careful, not sharing the same bed again until a trip to Key West three months after we met. We were so cautious and surreptitious that the announcement of our engagement a few weeks after the repeal of Don't Ask, Don't Tell caught by surprise everyone we knew.

My best man, a fellow pilot who had been less surprised by my coming out than I had expected, knocked on the door and poked his head in. "It's time."

I took one last look in the mirror and followed him to the staging area. Rather than either of us walking down the aisle, Scott and I approached the altar from either side and met in the middle. We stood before a church filled with family and friends as we professed our undying love, attended a simple reception following the ceremony and then drove to a hotel in the Dallas neighborhood of Oak Lawn to begin our life as a married couple.

The door of the honeymoon suite had barely closed behind the bellman when I pulled Scott into my arms and kissed him long and hard. Over the course of our developing relationship, we had kissed many times, but never like this, never as a married couple.

When the kiss ended, Scott took my hand, grabbed one of the small bags the bellman had piled just inside the door and led me into the bedroom. As I removed my uniform and hung it in the closet, Scott unpacked the bag and stripped off his suit. Wearing only my boxers, I turned my attention to the bed, where my new spouse awaited me beneath the covers. I kicked off my boxers and joined him there.

I braced myself on one elbow and gazed down into his eyes.

"I never thought this day would come," I said, as I stroked his cheek. A faint hint of five o'clock shadow sandpapered my thumb. "I never thought I could have a family *and* a military career."

I covered Scott's lips with mine before he could respond, and our kiss was longer and deeper than the one we'd shared when we'd first entered the honeymoon suite. I stroked his hair, ran my fingers down the length of his arm and cupped one asscheek in my palm, exploring his body almost as if it were our first time together.

Scott slipped a hand between us and wrapped his fist around my rising cock, gripping it like a joystick as he thumbed the tiny slit and smeared precum over the spongy-soft head.

Then he pushed aside the covers and kissed his way down my chest, over my taut abdomen to the neatly trimmed nest of hair at my crotch. My new spouse readjusted his position until he knelt between my widespread thighs and his warm breath tickled the head of my cock just before he wrapped his lips around it. As he pistoned his fist up and down the stiff shaft, he covered my cockhead with saliva, painting it with his tongue.

He slid his fist to the base of my cock and then took more

of my length into his mouth. From past experience I knew the entire length was more than he could handle but that didn't stop him from trying.

As he drew his head back, saliva escaped and slid down the length of my shaft to dampen the thatch of hair at my crotch and tickle my ball sac. He cupped my balls with his free hand and kneaded my nuts. When his teeth caught on the ridge of my swollen glans, he reversed direction. He stopped kneading my nuts and tickled the sensitive spot behind my nut sac, his finger sliding backward until it pressed against the tight pucker of my sphincter.

He moved his head up and down, faster and faster, pressing ever more firmly against my sphincter with his unlubed finger.

I couldn't restrain myself and soon my hips were bucking up and down on the bed. I wrapped my fingers in Scott's hair and thrust upward to meet his face each time it descended.

Then, just as I was about to cum, my ass relaxed and Scott's finger slid into me and pressed against my prostate. I came and came hard, once again propelling a thick wad of hot spunk against the back of Scott's throat.

He swallowed every drop before he released my cock and slid up the bed into my arms. I'm not usually quick to rebound, but this was our wedding night and soon my cock rose again.

Scott had unpacked the lube while I had been undressing and it was on the nightstand. After I slathered some on my reenergized cock, I squeezed a glob on my middle fingers and slid my hands between his thighs and under his ball sac. I massaged his sphincter until I could slip one finger into Scott's ass, and I continued massaging it until I could slip in a second finger.

When I knew he was ready, I removed my fingers and rolled on top of my new spouse. I pulled his knees up until he could hook his legs over my shoulders. Then, with his erect cock trapped between us, I drove my cock into his well-lubed ass and stared into his eyes as I made love to him.

As I slowly pistoned my cock in and out of Scott's ass, my abdomen rubbed the underside of his erect cock. Our sex started slow and easy but soon grew hard and fast.

My new spouse came first, covering my abdomen and his with sticky cum. Then I came, sending my second wad of hot spunk deep inside him. I collapsed atop him and didn't move until I'd caught my breath and my softening cock finally slipped free.

After we lay together for a bit, Scott said, "I'm hungry but I don't think I want to leave the bed any time soon."

"I can take care of that," I told him. I reached for the room service menu and we examined it together. A moment later I rolled over, reached for the phone and dialed room service. As soon as the call was answered, I said, "My husband and I would like—"

I hesitated, unexpectedly choked up. Scott and I had been married less than a day, but it was the first time I had ever referred to him as my husband. I looked over at Scott—at my husband—and felt as if I was soaring higher than I'd ever soared before without ever leaving the ground.

"Sir?" asked the voice on the other end of the line.

I kissed Scott and then completed placing our order.

My husband and I had a glorious future ahead of us.

CANDY MAN

Gregory L. Norris

Twenty kilometers from the Pakistan border, northwest of the Khyber Pass, northeast of the bombed-out remains of Tora Bora, Firebase Phoenix, one of the most hard-fought areas in Afghanistan, seemed at the farthest end of the universe.

Inside the fortified living quarters, Weare turned the corner and continued forward toward the room at the end of the corridor that would be home for the duration of this tour. A lone figure exited the room and approached. Weare froze where he stood.

The man was older now, with silver showing in the neat buzz of his dark hair, especially above both ears. "You," he said around the lollypop stick hanging at a lazy angle from one corner of his mouth.

The lone word roused Weare from the spell of thoughts he'd fallen under, and vanquished years of regret. Heat raced through his blood, and his body woke from a long sleep. Red rose on his throat and cheeks. His cock stirred in his BDUs and threw itself against his underwear and button-fly. For the first time in days—maybe months—Weare smiled.

"Yeah," he said.

What passed next between them did so through a kind of telepathy. Without warning or preparation, Weare spiraled back through time and was there again, in that brief but wonderful chapter of his secret past.

PFC Jeremy Weare made a promise to himself during the tense flight from Germany: he would hold on to the best memories, the best smells and tastes from home, once they hit the sand. He didn't have a lot to draw upon; his personal highlight reel, at twenty-four, wasn't jam-packed with a life's worth of *kapow* moments. But he hoped what he brought with him in spirit would be enough.

Everything was different over there, and no amount of bullshitting or briefing prepared him for exactly how vast the shift went from familiar to foreign. Weare told himself that the turkey and mashed potatoes served in the mess hall really were like the best Thanksgiving meals from that other time and place, *B.I.*—Before Iraq. And that the fake tree with the cheap paper decorations and twinkling lights represented a real holiday. But at night, when Weare slept, if he slept, his mind drifted back to rural Maine, and, sometimes, he caught a phantom hint of sap pine before waking in a strange land where nothing made sense, a million miles from home.

Secretly, he played a private game when not dodging bullets or roadside explosives. For every new, terrible memory being indelibly recorded, he called up a better one and accentuated the positive. Weare didn't want to be here in the heat, the filth, or the increasingly hostile climate, but he convinced himself he did, else he wouldn't have signed up to make the world safer when one of his buddies was taking a full ride on a football scholarship and another, Donald, was working his family's farm, likely spending long days sawing down Christmas trees that smelled of the holiday, sweet and alive.

One shower a week, if that. He looked at the time between as a way to conserve the bar of soap he'd brought with him from Maine—green, a real man's brand according to the commercials. With his back to the rest of the men, Weare soaped up his balls, lathered his cock and jerked himself almost to completion, knowing his fellow warriors were engaged in a similar ritual, satisfying a required need destined to be repeated in the barracks after lights out. Maybe they, too, thought of pumpkin pie and cinnamon as a way to stay strong; peppermint candy canes, and turkey stuffing that was moist and savory, not tasteless and hard enough to shoot out of a tank's boom stick.

He was showering, fantasizing of chocolate-covered cherries and the best sex of his young life, a few pumps shy of blasting his seed down the drain, where it would join the loads of so many other American infidels, eventually making it into the desert's water table, when the scuffle of slides drew Weare's gaze toward his right. The stall space beside him was no longer empty. Another male body, naked save the slides, ambled up to the nozzle, turned on the water and ducked into its rare, cleansing spray. Around the scent of his soap, Weare detected a man's sweat—that mix of the fresh and athletic along with the ripe from balls and feet, armpits and asshole. And something else. Something *sweet*.

That was Weare's first encounter with the new lieutenant, Christopher Collins.

He unconsciously drew a deep breath. Cherry? Taking a bold glance up, Weare noticed the lollypop stick hanging out of the other man's unshaved mouth. Dude smelled like home.

* * *

Collins joined him at the table in the mess, and introductions were made. Freshly scrubbed and smelling the way manly Irish men were expected to, Weare picked at the pasta and meat sauce, moving the food around with his fork more than actually eating it. Pretending this slop was as good as the spaghetti and meatball dinners on cold, snowy nights in Maine almost worked—until he caught Collins staring, and Weare gazed up, connecting with the other man in a way that was both thrilling and devastating at the same time.

"Thanks for the loan of your soap in there. So, where you from?" Collins asked, his voice a deep, charming drawl from some point on the map between the Blue Ridge Mountains and the bayou.

Weare told him. "Not much there but pinecones and rocks."

He didn't mention that he was narrowly ahead of a tidal wave of misery over missing the world he knew while following his marching orders in this alien realm. He sensed he didn't need to, because Collins got it.

"Hey, L-T, you gonna eat your pasta or jerk off into it," one of the guys at the table joked, his mouth full of food.

"Already beat off—into yours, Thomas," Collins fired back.

Thomas expelled a mouthful of his meal to a cacophony of good-natured chuckles. In that one sentence, Collins did more to lighten the general mood than anything Weare had managed on his own. He liked this dude, who'd caught him looking in the shower and had asked to borrow his soap. Oh yeah. A lot.

There was much about the dude to like. Hell, to love. And you didn't have to search too hard for the reasons.

Collins wasn't tall—he measured somewhere around five-eight. But he was big in other ways besides simple physical height. His smile, for starters—Collins would grin, sometimes snarl, revealing a length of perfect white teeth.

"Don't get too jealous, *amigos*," he drawled the next time Weare and he crossed paths in the showers. Collins stood at the sink in his slides and a towel, flossing. "I got a mean sweet tooth, so these pearly whites'll be dropping out of my mug any day now."

His teeth. His handsome face and classic jaw, which showed perpetual five o'clock shadow, regardless of the time of day. Tight, muscled body. And his scent, which Weare loved—a man's sweat mixed with something sweet. Candy.

On patrol through Tikrit, Weare stole another hit of the lieutenant's smell and soon understood its source: Collins had a bag of candy in his pocket, another stored in his ruck. American candy. Kisses and lollypops and little chocolate bars. Candy from home.

Finally, it all made perfect sense. The candy wasn't just to satisfy one man's personal sweet tooth. There was another mission, one beyond patrolling streets and maintaining a fragile peace that seemed destined to unravel and would in the weeks ahead.

Collins strutted at a safe distance from the civilians, called out something in Arabic, and was mobbed by local kids, who streamed over to him, speaking in excited voices.

"Candy! Candy!"

He doled out the chocolate bars and gumballs.

"You gotta win their hearts if you want to win the war," he said to Weare.

The man was a genius. And by then he sure had won Weare's heart.

* * *

When he was younger, one of Weare's favorite things to drink was chocolate milk. You squeezed syrup into a tall glass, poured in cold whole milk, stirred it with a spoon and drank the concoction through a twisty Krazy Straw. You couldn't reuse the straw for long, as the things tended to grow rank as the milk residue trapped inside soured. But there was something magical about that simple recipe. It defied words, logic. It was one of Weare's happiest memories.

Weare mentioned it in passing to Collins during one of the lieutenant's goodwill missions. The other man flashed a cocky smirk, and Weare melted on the inside, his pulse driven into a gallop by Collins's shades, his unshaved face and the lollypop stick hanging out of that smile full of clean white teeth.

A week later, Weare found a package sitting on his bunk. He opened the simple brown wrapper and couldn't believe what waited inside. Not only had Collins gotten him a bottle of chocolate syrup, the real stuff from home, but a twisty straw as well.

"Dude," Weare sighed, "are you for real?"

"Maybe. No thanks though, little buddy."

When Weare did anyway, Collins grabbed him in a playful headlock and kissed the top of Weare's buzz cut.

"I said," he drawled, "think nothing of it. Seriously, the pleasure was all mine."

Night fell. Snores filled the barracks following lights out.

"Hey, dude," Collins whispered.

Weare sat up to find the other man seated on the edge of his bottom bunk. "Huh?"

"Shhh," Collins said, with a sweet breath that smelled of mint.

Weare drew in a deep lungful. Among the scent, he detected maleness, fresh sweat, musk. He'd woken hard and quickly grew stiffer. "What is it, man?"

"This," Collins answered.

And then the new lieutenant leaned down and crushed their mouths together. The kiss was sweet in taste, bitter in concept because it was also forbidden. Weare tensed, broke their liplock and cast a worried glance around the barracks room filled with sleeping phantoms.

"I thought…" Collins said, and moved away.

The distance grew to what felt like kilometers. Weare panicked—more from the fear of losing Collins, less over worries of being found out. "You thought right."

Weare hooked a hand around the lieutenant's neck and pulled him back. This kiss was equally awkward and verged on painful, but necessary in painting them both as criminals guilty of the same crime. Collins's tongue tested Weare's boundaries. Weare opened wider, inviting access. A low, happy growl rose up from the other man's throat. Weare's hand slipped down and caressed the rough stubble of cheek, chin and throat en route to the lieutenant's chest.

"Dude," Collins sighed. "I can't fucking stand this. Not another second."

"I know. I want you, too, man."

"Well, here I am. Let's you and me do this, all right?"

Collins's touch boldly sought other flesh. Weare bit back a moan as fingers walked over his stomach and under the elastic waistband of his underwear. Collins gripped his cock, and Weare worried he'd either come from that connection alone or pass out.

"You like that?" Collins taunted in a lusty whisper.

Weare muttered an affirmative.

"If that's so, you best prove it, dude."

Collins released his grip and straightened. Before he could think clearly, Weare reached for the other man's crotch. The front of Collins's shorts stood tented in the near dark. Weare tugged downward. The lieutenant's erection snapped out—an uncircumcised beaut wreathed in dark curls, with two fat balls hanging loose and full beneath. No more lusting from afar in the showers; Collins was his, all his. And he was the lieutenant's.

Collins planted a hand on top of Weare's head and guided him down. Lips met cockhead and noose of foreskin. A funky tang ignited on Weare's tongue.

"Suck it," Collins urged. "Oh, dude, suck my fucking dick..."

The smell, the taste, was as much *home* to Weare as Thanksgiving dinners and Christmas trees, candy bars and ice-cold watermelon at the height of August dog days, the fragrance of mowed summer lawns and the smoky haze in the air that telegraphs snowstorms are on their way during long, cold Maine winters.

He opened wider and swallowed the other soldier's cock deeper, almost to the balls. Those he tickled, rolling the meaty pair around in their sac and stirring their sweaty smell.

"Oh fuck, yeah, keep doing that, dude," Collins sighed.

Weare tugged. Collins responded with a grunt and shifted on the lower bunk. Weare sucked harder, faster. The sleeping bodies elsewhere in the dark added a level of excitement he hadn't dreamed possible. But on this night, all things *were*.

The taste of the lieutenant's precome strengthened. Nothing, Weare thought, could make this memory better, because eventually the sun would rise and they'd still be in this arid wasteland superimposed over the same space as the cradle of civilization, and neither man would be able to speak about the rebirth of sorts that had happened here because of rules, regulations and rhetoric over what could be asked or told.

Liquid warmth exploded across Weare's tongue, salty and slightly sweet. Weare swallowed it down. The pressure and hot male stink in the air intensified. Time froze. The world held its breath.

Eventually, Collins spoke. "Turn around."

Weare exhaled and shifted on the bunk. "What—?"

"Trust me."

Collins yanked down the younger man's shorts, baring his ass to warm breaths and more of those possibilities. Before Weare could comment or protest, cool, dense liquid drizzled over his most private flesh. Joy replaced worry. Weare shoved his face into his pillow to bury the laughter.

After setting down the bottle of chocolate syrup, Collins lowered his mouth to Weare's asshole and feasted.

Now they stood together in a different country, a different time and political climate. They were the same men, however.

Collins smiled. "You're here."

"Couldn't keep me away," Weare said. "And now that I am...no more secrets. No more lies."

"Great to see you," Collins said.

Weare leaned closer. "Truly, dude. I've missed you. Oh, how much..."

Collins reached into his front pocket. The motion of his fingers captured Weare's focus, and his mind drifted. From that wonderland between his legs, Collins produced a fresh lollypop and handed it over. Cherry. "Welcome home."

Weare accepted the gift. Home? It sure felt like it.

SEMPER FI
WRESTLERS

Bearmuffin

Master Sergeant Bill O'Conner couldn't think of a better job to have than to be wrestling in the Marines. He got to coach hunky, muscular wrestlers every day and traveled to bases around the world recruiting studs for the United States Marine Corps All-Marine Wrestling Team.

This month he was at the wrestling camp at Camp Pendleton in San Diego County. The All-Marine team was reestablished each year with tryouts, "wrestle-offs" that were held to see who would ultimately make the team. More than anything he wanted to have an all-gay team that he could be proud of.

Now that it was cool to be gay in the military, he was able to recruit more openly gay wrestlers to the fold. He was fifty and had been a Marine since he was twenty-five. He remembered the old days of military homophobia and now with the new freedoms he would be able to hook up with other like-minded athletic studs without fear of reprisal.

His confidence and innate wisdom, in addition to his natural authoritative and commanding presence, inspired a kind of old-fashioned hero worship in his men. Old-fashioned in the sense that it would not be going too far to say that Master Sergeant O'Conner elicited the kind of undying allegiance and love known in ancient times in Greece or Rome.

He was tall and built like a tackle, all of it pure solid muscle. Not only did he have a football player's rugged good looks but his chin was strong, his jaw angular. His crew cut was razor sharp. His deep-set dark eyes, thick brows and trimmed mustache made him the perfect Marine Daddy, especially with that distinguished touch of gray at the temples.

And no one appreciated a daddy more than Sergeant Tom Hansen, from Boise, Idaho.

Sergeant Hansen stood three inches shorter than O'Conner's six-foot-two. Even so, he had a sizzling symmetrical physique. He was Ivy League handsome with brown hair flecked with gold. His eyes were a pale blue and they enhanced his dazzling smile. O'Conner was beside himself with lust and wanted to kiss Sergeant Hansen's mouth for hours. He wanted to stick his tongue down Hansen's throat, grab his buns of steel and hold him tight. Then O'Conner would rub his hefty cock all over Hansen's amazing, ripped midsection and spooge all over those hard-as-steel six-pack abs.

O'Conner went crazy watching Hansen wrestle. O'Conner wanted to wrestle that six-pack-abbed, hard-bodied hunk so bad he could taste Hansen's jockstrap sweat. Yeah, he'd pin Hansen. He'd grab his thick thighs, spread them apart and suck his asshole for hours. Then O'Conner would sit on Hansen's face and let him rim him. Then he'd fuck the living daylights out of Sergeant Hansen.

The feeling was mutual. Hansen instantly noted the black fur fanning over O'Conner's broad pecs and he could see tufts of it poking out through the neck hole of O'Conner's regulation white T-shirt stretched over his barrel chest. His thick nipples tented his shirt. He was attracted to O'Conner's mesmerizing masculinity, his powerful erotic charisma.

Hansen saw how O'Conner's blue gym trunks exposed his hairy, burly legs. O'Conner's jockstrap peeped out over the waistband of his shorts. Many a time Hansen had fantasized about getting O'Conner's jockstrap, sniffing it and jacking off while he tripped out on O'Conner's ripe, masculine smells.

The Marine wrestling camp was two months long. Naturally, hard-core physical training and wrestling were involved that pushed the wrestlers to their limits. They really had to prove to O'Conner that they had what it took to be an All-Marine wrestler. And if a hot and sweaty practice bout led to some hot man-to-man action on or off the mat that was all the better.

Three pairs of wrestlers grappled on the mats, scuffling and groaning, their hot young bodies streaked with sweat. Within minutes the gym was permeated with the arousing odor of manly jock-sweat. The stench excited O'Conner. His cock twitched and his balls rumbled with lust. With a pair of alert, narrowed eyes, O'Conner watched Hansen wrestle Corporal Smith.

O'Conner was thrilled with Smith's beefy farm-boy masculinity. Smith was a tower of solid muscle slabbed onto his perfectly proportioned frame, which was highlighted by great pecs and washboard abs. His light brown hair was streaked with gold. His killer smile and cobalt blue eyes instantly mesmerized everyone. Smith hailed from Minnesota.

Endless hours in the gym had honed Smith's muscular frame to spectacular perfection. The nineteen-year-old stud sported a tight, hard bubble butt that took your breath away, even more so when it was framed by the straps of a white jock that emphasized the deep, rich tan of his smooth skin. Smith always wore his jockstrap a size too small. He loved the way it lewdly displayed his meaty cock and big balls.

O'Conner's heart thumped whenever he got a gander at the young wrestler's hot pecs, powerful muscles and terrific bubble butt stuffed inside his wrestling singlet. Smith had thick nipples, the kind that O'Conner could chew on for a week.

As O'Conner watched Corporal Smith grapple with Sergeant Hansen, he became more agitated. He couldn't resist squeezing the ever-thickening bulge inside his jockstrap.

O'Conner could always tell when a couple of wrestlers were fucking each other. Yeah. He was sure of it. Smith and Hansen were fuckbuddies!

Now he really wanted to get a finger up Smith's hot bubble butt. O'Conner rubbed his crotch some more, then he adjusted his jockstrap, pulling the sweat-soaked pouch away from his thick cock and turgid balls.

Suddenly, O'Conner noticed that Smith was staring at him. Smith's wolfish grin intrigued the coach. O'Conner smiled. Studs were naturally attracted to his magnificent virile beauty. He exuded such machismo that the testosterone bounced off the walls. The whole room could sense the power.

O'Conner was getting hornier by the minute. He needed to pop his wad. So he wasn't going to waste any more time. Practice was about over anyway. O'Conner blew his whistle.

"Okay, men," he barked. "Showers!"

Smith and Hansen were walking toward the locker room but O'Conner stopped them with an authoritative hand.

"Smith, you stay here. Work on your takedowns. They're sloppy."

Hansen joined the other studs in a mad rush to the showers. O'Conner immediately noticed how Smith's crotch was bulging.

He'd popped a huge boner wrestling with Hansen and it poked out, lewdly tenting his singlet.

"Okay," O'Conner said, pointing to the mat. "Let's see a gut-wrench."

O'Conner and Smith wrestled. O'Conner quickly toppled Smith right on his sweet bubble-ass. O'Conner mashed his crotch against Smith's face on purpose, and chuckled when he felt it swell against the Corporal. He reached behind Smith and grabbed his ass. He rubbed his hands up and down Smith's ass, pushing the Lycra into his ass-crack. O'Conner jabbed his fingers inside Smith's ass, flipping the wrestler over in a perfect gut-wrench.

But O'Conner was surprised when Smith suddenly rallied and applied a hammerlock. O'Conner could hardly breathe because Smith had pressed his crotch right on his face.

O'Conner felt Smith's cock swell up against his face. Purposefully, O'Conner jabbed his fingers harder into Smith's butt. Even though he had a singlet on, Smith could feel O'Conner's fingers invade his hole. He cried out with pain and lust. O'Conner's fingers wiggled inside his butt some more. O'Conner suddenly felt Smith's cock spasm and bolt and then shoot hot cum into his jock. There was so much cum, it seeped through both jock and singlet. O'Conner's face was soaked with Smith's potent cum.

O'Conner countered with a dazzling scissors hold right around Smith's neck. Once again he purposely mashed his groin against the young stud's face. O'Conner felt Smith's struggling body smashing against him, and Smith's muffled moans and groans blasting against his crotch. O'Conner was just too fucking strong for the lusty Smith who was trying to break free from the master sergeant's powerful hold.

All that rubbing and thrashing was giving O'Conner a major

hard-on. He ground his crotch all over Smith's face, until his cock throbbed harder than before. Suddenly, he cried out and spurts of cum exploded from his pisser, soaking through his singlet to drench Smith's astonished face with cum.

A triumphant O'Conner leaped up, gazing down at the defeated Smith.

"Next time, winner fucks the loser!"

Of course, it was more than just having sex for O'Conner. He wasn't a snob and paid no attention to rank, and he approached and enjoyed having sex with the men under his charge and treated them as equals. He truly loved them in every sense of the word and the newfound freedoms in the military made the enjoyment of homosexual love so much better in every way.

The next morning O'Conner was working out in the weight room.

He admired himself in the mirror. A clean, white jockstrap hugged his big cock and fat balls. He had just gunned off a few barbell sets. He started flexing and posing for his own amusement.

"Fuck!" O'Conner roared smugly. He was supremely pleased with his wonderfully muscled body. He ran a hand over his hard abs, relishing the feel of firm muscle under his sweaty palms. His blue eyes glowed with manly pride.

Sergeant Biff Stevens entered the room. O'Conner grinned, and his eyes flashed. The twenty-two-year-old sergeant stood tall. He had a powerful build, all of it pure muscle. He was from Montana. He had a shock of brown hair that fell over his forehead into his sexy brown eyes. His sharp, angular features were emphasized by a blunt nose with flared nostrils.

Sergeant Stevens wore regulation green gym shorts and a T-shirt. He was ready for a workout but didn't expect to run into O'Conner. All the same, he was proud to be under O'Conner's tutelage and Stevens's manly chest swelled with pride at the thought that he would do anything to please the older man, thoughts that made his cock bolt and his anal puckers twitch with anticipation.

Right now, O'Conner felt especially randy. He felt like blowing Sergeant Stevens's mind.

"These fucking glutes are so tight," O'Conner said. "I can stick a dime in them and you'd never be able to get it out."

Stevens's eyes widened, and his mouth fell open. He stood transfixed, his mind blown by the astonishing sight of a sweaty O'Conner wearing nothing but a jockstrap. O'Conner was truly an awesome specimen of butch manhood.

"Go ahead. Here's a dime." O'Conner tossed it to Stevens. "Stick it up my ass and I'll show you!"

Stevens was trembling. O'Conner grinned.

"Don't be scared," O'Conner said. "I won't bite!"

O'Conner laughed. Stevens was nervous, all right. O'Conner turned around, resting his palms on his knees. He thrust his butt out at Stevens. O'Conner felt a cool rush of air rustling the silky hairs trapped between his ass-cleft. "Go ahead," O'Conner barked. "Put it in!"

Stevens gulped, pulled back O'Conner's left buttock, and inserted the dime. He noticed that O'Conner's skin was smooth as satin. He could smell O'Conner's powerful masculine scent, which aroused him in spite of himself.

"Yeah!" O'Conner hissed when he felt Stevens's fingers brush his ass. If only Stevens would stick a finger up his ass. O'Conner's cock jerked at the thought.

Sergeant Stevens felt heavy-duty twinges assaulting his groin. An unexpected sensation of lust began to burn from deep within him, radiating throughout his body.

"Yeah," O'Conner hissed. "Look at those glutes." His back

was turned to Sergeant Stevens. O'Conner posed and flexed for
Stevens who was simply awestruck at this spectacular display
of muscle.

"Rock hard! Rock hard!" O'Conner roared.

He spun his head around and glared at Stevens, a challenging
grin on his kisser.

"Just try and get that sucker out!"

But Stevens wavered for a moment, so O'Conner lost his
customary cool.

"Do it!" he yelled, his lips twisting into an angry snarl.

Stevens placed both hands on each cheek. O'Conner's butt
was hard, solid, hot. O'Conner's intense body heat dazzled
Stevens. It felt sizzling to the touch.

Stevens tried to pry apart O'Conner's cheeks but, true to his
word, O'Conner kept the dime firmly clenched inside his ass.

Stevens finally gave up. "It's no use," he said.

"Give up?" O'Conner was triumphant. Stevens was speechless.

O'Conner suddenly bent over and let out a victorious cry
as the dime popped out from his ass, flew against the wall,
bounced off and ricocheted back to Stevens, landing right at his
feet. O'Conner's wild laughter echoed off the walls.

"Pretty neat trick, huh? Let's see you do it."

"I dunno, sir," Stevens said sheepishly.

"What's the problem?" O'Conner growled, glaring at Stevens
with narrowed eyes.

"Seems sort of silly," Stevens replied, surprised at his bold-
ness.

"Silly? Silly?" O'Conner's nostrils flared. "Nothing silly
around here unless I say so. You got that, Sergeant?"

"Yes, sir!" Stevens shouted instinctively, standing at attention.

"Fuckin' A Right!" O'Conner roared. "That's more like it. Now turn around and bend over!" Stevens was nervous, trembling, a drop of sweat trickling down his left temple. O'Conner was chuckling under his breath. He rubbed his hands all over Stevens's hard butt.

"Ya got nice glutes," O'Conner said.

Stevens felt his heart pumping, and his knees were shaking. He was wondering what O'Conner was going to do next. He clenched his buttocks together around O'Conner's finger. But O'Conner slapped Stevens's butt really hard. "Hold it, stud!"

O'Conner held his finger inside Stevens's butt, then he pressed it farther, probing until he reached the anal ring which was tight and impenetrable like a fortress. "Relax, stud," O'Conner ordered. He stuck his finger in the hole and popped it through the ring. Sergeant Stevens gasped when he felt O'Conner probing farther up his butthole until he reached his prostate.

O'Conner began massaging Stevens's prostate. Stevens gulped, and sweat streamed over his face. It was a first for Stevens. He was overwhelmed by the wonderful sensations elicited by O'Conner's strumming fingers. Stevens's cock began to twitch and swell in response to O'Conner's expertise.

"Sir?"

"Yeah?"

"Sir, I feel like," Stevens's voice trailed off. His face was beet red.

"Feel like what?" O'Conner chuckled to himself. He knew what was happening.

"If you keep that up, it feels like I'm gonna cum."

"Feels great, don't it?"

"Yes, sir."

"So I'll just keep on doing it. Okay with you?"

"Yes, sir."

O'Conner pressed himself against Stevens. His sweaty chest stuck to Stevens's broad back. His breath brushed against Stevens's earlobes. "You're one hot man," O'Conner whispered inside Stevens's ear. Stevens felt one of O'Conner's hands slide under his arm and begin to rub his abs.

As O'Conner ran a hand over Stevens's proud abs, he continued to massage Stevens's prostate. Stevens's head thrust backward, and his mouth flew open. His soft, lust-tinged sighs of pleasure gradually grew louder. O'Conner was playing with his abs now, rubbing the hard muscle with his hand. Then he caressed the firm mounds of his pecs.

"Hot pecs," O'Conner whispered into Stevens's ear.

The wrestler could smell O'Conner's salty body scent. It was exhilarating. Now Stevens's cock was hard, erect. O'Conner reached down and began to fondle it. He squeezed the shaft, and Stevens's hot veins pumped lustfully against his palm.

He moved down to cup the heavy balls and fondle them inside the scrotum. Stevens suddenly groaned, so O'Conner removed his fingers from Stevens's butt to begin playing with his nipples, first lightly nipping them with his fingernails and then squeezing the rubbery nuggets between his fingers.

"You take over," O'Conner whispered. He removed his hand from Stevens's balls. Stevens began to masturbate as O'Conner reinserted his fingers up Stevens's ass to continue massaging his prostate. With the other hand, O'Conner gingerly caressed Stevens's left pec.

O'Conner was playing Stevens like a piano. He knew how to trip him out, until each raw nerve felt like liquid fire. The sexual electricity was burning into Stevens's raw nerves until he could hold back no more.

Stevens was panting.

"Fuck! Oh, sir!"

"Yeah?"

Stevens clenched his eyes.

"Ah!"

"You're gonna shoot?"

Stevens's mouth was wide open.

"Aww!"

"Lemme see that wad!"

Stevens's muscles were quaking.

"Fuck!"

"Shoot that fucking load!"

"Unngh! Unngh!"

Stevens's nuts were aching for release. His breath escaped from his sensuous lips in ragged groans.

"Oh, fuck! Fuck! Fuck!"

"Yeah, stud! Shoot your load!"

Stevens arched back, smashing against O'Conner's broad chest.

"Shoot that load! Shoot it for me!"

Sergeant Stevens exploded, the cum rushing out of his cock, hitting the floor, splashing everywhere. His body went into hot spasms, slamming back against O'Conner's finger until the coach's knobby knuckles were digging deep against his crack. Stevens tossed his head back, his mouth open in an agonizing scream of pleasure, as he unleashed more of his cum. It shot forward in long thick spurts that arched up and splattered all over the floor.

"That was hot, stud!" O'Conner said.

Sergeant Stevens smiled.

"See ya at practice tomorrow!" O'Conner said.

O'Conner slipped on his sweats and sprinted out the door leaving Stevens to soak up the cum-streaked floor with his own jockstrap.

The next day, after a good solid hour of pumping iron, O'Conner went to the gym showers. He could always find some hot wrestler there to fuck.

Sure enough, Hansen was there lathering his big beefy body. So O'Conner stripped and joined him. O'Conner just reached up, going right for Hansen's meaty pecs. He rubbed Hansen's nipples between his fingers, pulling and tugging on those tender stud-nipples ever so gently. He flicked the edge of his fingernails over the tender tips of Hansen's nipples, making the young wrestler gasp with pleasure.

O'Conner was still horny. His puckers twitched. His cock bolted again. He wanted to fuck Hansen's ass.

"Bend over! I'm going to ream ya, son!" O'Conner barked.

Hansen grabbed the faucets as he bent over to expose his sweet ass for O'Conner's pleasure. Hansen thrust his butt against O'Conner's hard cock. O'Conner rubbed the knobby head along Hansen's puckers.

O'Conner groaned. "Like that?"

"Yes, sir!"

"Ya love my cock against your ass, son?"

"Yes, sir!"

"Ya got such a hot body." O'Conner's hands were running all over Hansen's wet body. "So fucking hot."

O'Conner loved to see the fine golden hairs whorling on Hansen's hot ass. He ran his hands over each cheek, the silk gliding under his rough hands.

O'Conner whispered in Hansen's ear, his lips brushing against Hansen's peach fuzzed earlobe. "I want to fuck you, Hansen."

"Yeah."

"You want me to, don't you, Hansen?

"Oh yeah, Coach. Yeah!"

O'Conner placed a hand over Hansen's abs. He felt the excitement surging through Hansen's sweating body. O'Conner wrapped his hand around the horny wrestler's cock. It bobbed wildly as O'Conner continued to whisper hypnotically into Hansen's ear, his hot breath mingling with the wrestler's heavy sighs.

"I'm gonna fuck you, Sergeant. Good and slow."

O'Conner squeezed Hansen's cock. It throbbed with lust.

"Gonna put my cock up your ass."

"Right, sir!"

"I'm gonna ram my fuckin' cock up your ass!"

"Right, sir! Do it!" Hansen anxiously wiggled his butt back and forth. "Fuck my hole!"

O'Conner teased Hansen's puckers with the spasming knob of his cock. He circled it along Hansen's twitching hole, coating it with precum. Hansen gasped with macho pleasure, hoping that O'Conner would fuck him good and hard.

Be careful what you wish for, you'll usually get it.

Because O'Conner plunged his cock right inside Hansen's hole.

Hansen screamed, he wailed. O'Conner was ramming into his butt.

"You're getting fucked. Fucked real good!"

O'Conner laughed when Hansen tried to wrench himself free. O'Conner continued to plunge his cock up Hansen's ass. He felt his cockveins swell with lust, searing Hansen's butthole.

"Unngh, unngh," Hansen grunted. "Please, sir. Please cum now." He desperately wanted O'Conner to shoot his wad.

"Ya want it now?"

"Yeah, give it to me. Shoot your load!"

O'Conner's mega-muscles suddenly went taut. He clenched his eyes and his tongue waggled to and fro.

O'Conner screamed a deep macho groan as the first load of white-hot cum streamed out of his cock right into Hansen's spasming asshole. Hansen cried out, pushing his ass back, as O'Conner's balls crashed against the root of his cock, making him cum too, sending spurt after spurt of cum splashing on the tiles.

Sergeant Hansen finished showering and left.

O'Conner closed his eyes and let the water rush over his muscles. That's when mega-muscled Corporal Lance Burton ambled in.

O'Conner watched Corporal Burton lather his magnificent cock. Burton was still wearing his jockstrap. O'Conner grinned but he didn't think it was strange at all. Sometimes the wrestlers did that, keeping their jocks on and washing them in the shower room as they soaped up their cocks and balls.

Burton's cock was thirteen inches long, three inches thick. The lusty twenty-four-year-old South Dakotan certainly sported one of the biggest cocks O'Conner had ever seen. O'Conner knelt on the slippery shower floor, positioning himself between Corporal Burton's tree trunks. He leaned forward to pull down the blond wrestler's jockstrap. Burton's cock swelled obscenely, popping out of the pouch, smacking O'Conner right in the kisser.

O'Conner had a great view of Corporal Burton's magnificently rugged body. Tiny golden hairs swirled deliciously around his thick, golden brown nipples. O'Conner licked his lips as his greedy eyes followed the faint trail of hair running from Burton's belly button down below the wide waistband of his jock circling his taut waist. When O'Conner pulled down the waistband, Burton's mammoth cock sprang up like a well-oiled machine.

"Ya like that stud meat, don'tcha, sir?" Burton said. He was so very cocky, but the master sergeant liked it.

He leered at Burton with lusty green eyes. "Yeah, I sure fucking do."

Burton relished the situation. O'Conner was on his hands and knees, begging for cock.

"Whatcha waitin' for then, huh? Go for it, sir," Burton rasped.

So O'Conner took the famous thirteen inches in his left hand and ran his right hand through Burton's silky, golden-hued pubes.

With both hands, O'Conner began to pump Burton's cock. O'Conner was filled with awe as Burton's foreskin slid up and down the shaft, first covering his knob then stretching it below the glans. O'Conner marveled at the wet, slapping sound of the skin slithering over Burton's blue cockveins.

O'Conner's eager tongue slid out of his wet mouth and flickered over the tip of Burton's proud cock. A thick drop of precum glistened brazenly inside the pisshole.

Burton's precum tasted tangy, rich. And with that fantastic cum-taste still fresh in his anxious mouth, O'Conner ran his tongue down the side of his cock and flickered over his golden balls. They were permeated with a powerful, manly odor. The smell rushed up O'Conner's nose, dilating his nostrils, making him heady with desire.

O'Conner then made his way back to Burton's knob, running his tongue all around the precum-dripping pisshole. Burton grabbed O'Conner's head and pushed him down over his turgid meat. O'Conner sucked cock like never before.

Corporal Burton's hands gripped O'Conner's head, making sure his cock stayed inside O'Conner's mouth.

"Yes, sir. Suck that cock! Suck it, you cocksucker. SUCK IT!!"

What an incredible sight. O'Conner was Corporal Burton's

suck slave. O'Conner enjoyed every minute. Corporal Burton laughed as he pumped his mighty cock between O'Conner's sputtering lips.

"Awwww, awwwww, suck it, sir, suck it!"

O'Conner massaged Burton's big, sweaty, cum-filled balls.

"Yeah, that's it. My balls!"

O'Conner played with Burton's balls some more.

Suddenly, Burton arched back. He opened his mouth and cried out, "Fuck!"

One, two, three, four, five steamy cumspurts careened down O'Conner's spasming throat. O'Conner grabbed his own spasming cock, shooting a hot load that flew up between them and splattered on the ceiling.

O'Conner fell back on his butt. He was breathless, with hot cum dribbling down his face. But when he looked up at Burton he instantly noticed the wild look in Burton's baby blues. Yeah! Burton wanted to fuck some more.

Burton shoved O'Conner's legs apart. Greedily, he swallowed O'Conner's cock. He began to suck off O'Conner at a fierce tempo. Burton's mouth bobbed up and down on O'Conner's cock with an amazing dexterity. Burton's hands roamed all over O'Conner's humpy butt. With a lustful wink, he wiggled a finger up O'Conner's ass. O'Conner was delighted, humming his manly pleasure.

Burton rolled O'Conner over on his stomach. He jumped behind O'Conner, wrenching his asscheeks apart so he could eat ass. Corporal Burton rimmed O'Conner for a while. The master sergeant was in heaven. He loved how Corporal Burton was sucking his ass.

After giving O'Conner a thorough rim job, Burton decided to fuck him.

O'Conner winced because Burton's cock was so fucking

hard, so fucking big! Even so, Burton managed to work his knob past O'Conner's anal ring. Sensing that O'Conner had relaxed, Burton worked his cock up O'Conner's hole. Soon, his golden pubes were tickling O'Conner's ass.

"Fuck!" O'Conner cried out. Waves of lust surged through his muscles. He felt a powerful, mind-boggling bliss. The kind you get when a hot stud is reaming you with thick, fat cock.

"Take it, sir. Take my fucking cock! Take it!"

O'Conner loved it. He was being used and abused by this big Marine jock. Later, he'd turn the tables. But for now he'd sit back and enjoy the ride.

"Unngh, unngh, unngh!" O'Conner listened to Corporal Burton's loud grunts while for ten solid minutes, Burton brutally ass-fucked his coach. Finally, when O'Conner couldn't take any more, he begged Burton to shoot.

"So you want it, sir?"

"Yeah!"

"Want my load?"

"Yeah, gimme that load. Shoot it up my ass!"

Burton pushed forward with a rebel yell and sunk his cock all the way up O'Conner's butt. O'Conner screamed, his cock exploding, cum gushing from his pisshole.

"Fuck!!"

Burton shot an endless stream of cum. It seemed as if Burton's cock would never stop shooting. Finally, it did.

Burton popped his cock from O'Conner's hole. He showered, dressed and prepared to leave for class, and so did O'Conner, but not before planting an ardent kiss on Burton's lovely mouth. Burton caressed O'Conner's firm, muscular body. And the master sergeant returned the gesture. They were both filled with homoerotic passion, a passion that would have to be satisfied the next time they met.

And so, stud by stud, O'Conner seduced his team of studs until he had gathered together a team that was truly a force to be reckoned with. They were lean, mean and Marine Corps green, twenty gay studs ready to kick some ass and capture some glory for the Corps. *Semper Fi!*

COMEUPPANCE

Rob Rosen

Three years to the day I returned to where I'd started from, Army Boot Camp 2.0, as I liked to call it. I'd been given a second chance to start from friggin' scratch. Goody for me. And, yes, bitter party, table for one. Still, at least I was finally invited inside the place, table and all.

Camp looked the same, smelled the same and felt the same, in fact. And me, I felt like last time as well, tummy rumbling, head pounding, eyes stinging from the heat and the sweat and the damned ever-present humidity. Yep, exactly the same, pretty much. Only, of course, it wasn't the same, not this time.

"Good to be back," I whispered to myself, swiping a hand across my drenched forehead. And, yes, I meant it, all things considered. Go figure.

I found my barracks easily enough, found my cot and my locker after that, and then, sad to say, found *him*. Goddamn Murphy's Law. "Sergeant," I said, standing at rest.

He gave me the onceover, twice, then half grimaced, half sneered. This guy was menace before Dennis had the title, hard as stone and twice as dense. "Thought we got rid of you, Malone," he grumbled, the sneer notching up a factor or two.

"You did, Sergeant," I replied, emphasis on the *you*, seeing as he was the one who turned me in, no asking, no telling. Just packed me up and shipped me out. And for what—a little blow job in my off hours that he found out about? Come on, give a guy a break already. "Guess it didn't stick too well," I added, upping his sneer with a wobbly smile that didn't seem to sit too kindly with him. Then again, it wasn't meant to.

"We'll see about that, Malone," he said between clenched jaws before moving down the aisle and away from yours truly, shaking his shaved head from side to side all the while.

And then I did flip him that bird after all. Felt good, too. Not nearly good enough, of course, but still. I even eyed that stellar ass of his, now that I sort of could do such a thing. At least when he wasn't looking.

Anyway, things got all boot campy pretty darn quick after that, all lock and load and what that entailed. In other words, soon enough, I was too pooped out to pay him much heed, apart from the mandatory shit that would only, thank goodness, last a short enough while. I'd pay my time and move on, I figured. There was nothing he could do about it this go around but grin and *bare* it.

Though he wasn't much of a grinner to start with.

The baring part remained to be seen, however. And surprisingly, in the middle of the night, not all that far into my training, came part *deux*.

See, I had a wicked need to pee that fateful evening, long after lights out, long after everyone was dead to the world, so much snoring as to make the tree frogs jealous. The latrine was out back, built some time when my daddy was an enlisted man. White cinder blocks, white tile, white ceiling and porcelain, all of it scrubbed to a blinding shine by lowly guys like me.

I entered the squat building, flicked the lights on and heard a shower come to a stop a heartbeat later, which was weird, seeing as everyone was sound asleep. Well, almost everyone, as it turned out.

"Malone," he grumbled, all of a sudden standing there, dripping from head to big-ass toe. Damn, pretty much all of him was big. *ALL* of him, if you get my drift. And all of him was what I was getting a gander at right about then. The gander *and* the goose, in fact. "Shouldn't you be in bed, Private?" he tossed in, wiping his broad expanse of muscle-dense chest with his towel, willie shaking in the reverse direction. "Didn't I work your ass hard enough today, or are you looking for more shit to do?"

I shook my head and gulped. "Just had to take a piss, Sergeant."

He waved his hand at me dismissively. "Then piss already, Private," he barked. "And stop your queer-ass staring."

I coughed and blinked. "You, um, you can't say stuff like that anymore, Sergeant." My belly suddenly tied up in knots, strong enough to dock a tanker with.

But he merely chuckled. "I can't, huh?" he said, towel moving to his tree-trunk-thick legs, balls the size of lemons dangling down, calves flexed, big as boulders. "You got any witnesses says I did such a thing?"

Now he had me pissed. Fucker. And with all that built-up adrenaline from the previous week boiling up, I strode the few feet that separated us, standing eye to eye with him all of a sudden. Or at least eye to chin. "I don't need any, Sergeant," I told him, voice about as steady as I could make it. "The Army says you can't call me that no more."

He dropped the towel and poked me in the chest. "Queer-ass," he repeated, steely eyes mere slits. "Queer-fucking-ass."

Well now, wouldn't you know it, but that adrenaline of mine bubbled the fuck on over at that one. Meaning, I punched him one in the chest. Hard, too. Or at least hard for me. Though it probably hurt my hand way more than his stupendously solid chest. "Don't call me that," I managed, dropping the *Sergeant* bit altogether.

He paused and stared down at the red that had managed its way across his chest, right where I'd socked him. Then, surprisingly, he smiled, teeth white and as straight as he was. "Queer-ass has some guts after all, huh?"

Again my fist went up and again it met flesh, and then again, sending him back an inch or two, both of us in shock at my seething outburst. Me especially, seeing as I could've sworn I heard him moan a bit at the second wallop, eyelids fluttering for the briefest of moments. "Stop it," I managed, panting now, legs suddenly shaky, throat dry.

"Or what?" he asked, again moving forward, chest out, eyes wide. "You'll tell mommy on me?" This time I backslapped his tummy, my hand going in the reverse direction on his dick. And I didn't imagine the moan or the eyelid flutter this time. Nope. Mainly because his dick swung and then kept right on swinging, arcing right before curving up, up and up some more. Sucker was a battering ram with only me in its path. Instinctively, I went to grab it, old habits dying hard, but he swatted my hand away. "Keep your queer mitts off of me, Private."

I retracted my hand, but still stayed firmly in place. "Says the man with the newfound kickstand." And to send the point home, I thwacked it again, sending it reeling, a mild breeze rising in its hefty wake.

Again he moaned, and said in reply, "Back to bed, Malone." Though it came out kind of weak, if you ask me.

This time I lifted both fists and punched both his pecs, the sound pinging in all directions, echoing off the tiled walls. "Not." *Pound.* "Tired." *Pound.* "Sergeant." And then I grabbed his eraser-tipped nipples and gave a hard tug and a ferocious tweak, which sent the mighty giant to his knees, the loudest moan yet escaping from between his lips, the sound swirling around us like a whipped-up cyclone.

He stared up at me, eyes again wide, hand suddenly yanking on his billy club of a prick, his free hand pointing at my fiercely tenting boxer shorts, which was all I was wearing at the time. "Lock the door, Private," he commanded, voice thick as molasses, those few words far greater than the sum of their parts.

I moved a couple of feet in reverse and slid out of my boxers, cock springing to life. "No witnesses, huh, Sergeant?"

"See," he said, still stroking his dick as he tossed in a wink for good measure. "You're not as stupid as you look, Private."

It was a backhanded compliment that earned him yet another backhand across his chest before I did as he'd said, turning to the door, which I locked up good and tight. When I turned around again, he was on all fours, butt facing my way, legs wide, balls low and bouncing as he jacked away. "And you are as big an *ass* as you look," I replied. "Sergeant." Which I meant quite literally, seeing as his solidly huge ass was beautifully beckoning me toward it.

I again closed the gap between us, sitting cross-legged directly behind him, praying to the altar, as it were. And my tithing was a hard smack across his buttcheek, then another, both yielding moans in praise, his hand picking up speed on his dick, which I figured needed some attention on my part, too. So I grabbed his balls and gave a sharp tug up. He yelped, shuddered and released his pole, which was now pointing down to the tile below, translucent precome dripping off the mushroom-wide head. I pulled harder on his nut sac, and the shudder repeated, rolling over his entire body like waves at the shoreline. "Slap it, Private," he grunted, turning his thick neck my way.

Well, seeing as he wasn't specific, I slapped it all: left cheek, right cheek, hole and balls and dick, repeatedly, until everything was beet red, with a little cayenne thrown in for flavor.

By then, I was drenched with sweat and my cock was so thick in my grip that I thought it would explode at any moment. Still, I wasn't done with him. Three years of anger needed to come out. On him. Three years with interest, no less, and at a rate the banks would've killed for.

"Roll over, Sergeant," I then told him. He didn't reply or move, just remained there, jacking merrily away. "Or the party's over."

He sighed and grunted, clearly not accustomed to being told what to do, at least by the likes of me. Still, he relented, little head clearly in charge of the big head. Not that either were all that little, mind you. In any case, down he went to the floor, then over, body splayed out, eyes on me and mine on him. A buffet of flesh, meat and potatoes for days. "Well, Private?" he said, cock in hand again, a slow stroke beginning as he waited for the next onslaught.

I grinned and spanked his chest, harder, harder, hardest. "Feet up and hold 'em up."

"Sergeant," he cautioned.

I shrugged. "Fine, feet up and hold 'em up, *Sergeant*."

He nodded and complied, his feet lifted above his midsection, knees wide, hands holding them there. I was now on the ground at his side, one hand stroking my rigid prick, the other spanking his hairy exposed hole, over and over again, each time eliciting a grunt or a groan, a gasp or a sigh. "More," he managed, eyes shut tight, mouth in a determined snarl, fist moving like lightning on his club of a cock.

So more is what he got, my palm spanking away as I leaned down, face to face until I could smell the soap he'd just scrubbed with. "You like that asshole slapped by my queer hand, Sergeant? Like jacking off for your queer-ass Private?" He didn't reply; didn't need to really. The questions were, after all, rhetorical. And, I assumed, the answers were both yes and no. Not that I cared, because I, in fact, was having a grand old time of it. "Cat got your tongue, Sergeant?" I added, lifting my slapping hand to my mouth and hawking on it. Then I returned it to its target, a slow, steady glide of my slicked-up digits deep, deep inside of him. "Faggot got your ass, Sergeant?"

His back arched, his head was thrown back, and his body rumbled and shook as he loudly moaned out, "*Fuuuck.*"

Which is just what I did, pumping my double digits, soon triple, in and out, in and out, deep as I could go, rough as I could go, fast as I could go, until he was so wet with sweat himself that he was practically sliding on the tile now, still working his cock as I assaulted his tight-as-a-drum hole. "The Sergeant is a bottom," I chided. "Who would have guessed?"

He stopped pumping his prick and looked my way, the sneer once again evident on his sweat-soaked face. "Straight guys have prostates too, Private. Don't need to be queer to work it a little."

I shrugged and pushed in deeper, that prostate he mentioned getting ever harder beneath my constant prodding and pumping. "If you say so, Sergeant." Then I pulled out, a new twisted thought worming its way inside my head, one clearly more purposeful. "But maybe we can get us closer to the real deal than a few little fingers."

With his free hand, he punched my thigh, which hurt like a motherfucker. "No cocks up my ass, queer boy."

I jumped up and waved said cock, glorious as it was, down at

him. "Your loss, Sergeant, but I had another idea in that regard."
Actually, I had more than one, but it was only the one he got, for
the time being. And with us already in the latrine, I had a perfect
steely prick substitute for him. Emphasis on the steely.

Seconds later, I returned with a toilet-paper holder from
one of the stalls. Six inches and hard, it would do in a pinch.
And that it did, lubed with hand soap, and sliding forcibly up
his rump. "Mmm," he sighed as I slid it on home. "Mmm," he
moaned again as I turned it clockwise inside of him.

"Now, Sergeant, go fuck yourself," I told him, with a chuckle,
jumping up as the metal tube hung there, suspended half in, half
out of his hole. Needless to say, he picked up where I'd left off,
fucking himself and jacking away, body writhing on the floor
while I sat off to the side of him again, plucking his nipples like a
harp, my cock in my hand, watching, waiting, biding my time.

"Close," he soon enough rasped, panting, eyes squinting,
sweat pooling on the floor.

"Wait!" I shouted, then caught myself. "I mean, one more
thing, Sergeant. Because, come on, that thing up your ass is
puny; you probably can't even feel it. Let me go get something
even better. I promise you'll get a bigger, um, *kick* out of it." Or
at least one of us would.

He stopped his jacking, thick prick standing at attention.
Fuck, I almost saluted the damned thing. He eyed me suspiciously, but nodded just the same. "No cocks, queer-ass," he
spat, wiping a river of perspiration off his face as he continued
fucking himself, his pace slowing down just a bit for now.

"No cocks, Sergeant," I promised, hopping up as I quickly
slid my boxers back on. "Be right back. Then it's coming time."
Or at least comeuppance.

"Hurry, Malone," he grunted, swollen stiffie again in hand
as he watched me unlock the latch and rush outside.

I smiled as I shut the door behind me, waiting for my prick to go semi again. "Oh, I'll hurry, Sergeant," I whispered, head turning from side to side as I sought out my opportunity. "I mean, I've been waiting three long years for this, don't want to wait another minute longer."

Thankfully, less than a minute was all I needed, too. I mean, the military police are pretty easy to find, and they act rather quickly when you tell them you heard weird noises coming from the latrine. Oh, and perhaps added a little fib about seeing someone who looked sort of smarmy milling about. Maybe in some sort of foreign garb.

In other words, they took off running, rifles at the ready, me about twenty feet behind, not wanting to miss a moment of the festivities.

I had a ringside seat, too. Off to the side of the latrine was the ventilation unit; I just had to hop up and gaze in. And, man, what a sight it was to see, especially with my cock pulled out of my boxers, finally ready for some much-needed release. It and me both.

The MPs rushed in, guns extended, fingers at the ready. They didn't find no suspicious foreigner either, just a naked, hard, jerking sergeant with a toilet paper holder jammed deep up his ass. Sucker went flying out like a newly lit rocket as he jumped up, cock swaying, looking much like a deer caught in the head-lights, or a scared jackrabbit, minus the jacking, which he was officially done with right about then.

Suffice it say, that image of him standing there, defenseless, naked, hard and dripping with sweat, now of the flop variety; that was all I needed. My knees buckled some then, I tossed my head back, and a rumble went up from my lungs and out from between my lips. The moan carried on the sticky night air as I spewed and spewed and spewed some more, thick wads of white spunk hitting the equally white cement before sliding down, every nerve ending in my body shooting off Fourth of July fireworks.

"Guess you got your witnesses after all, Sergeant," I panted as I stuffed my prick back inside my boxers and hopped down before returning to my waiting cot, which, strangely enough, was just about the most comfortable bed I'd ever slept in all of a sudden. See, Army Boot Camp might've been 2.0, but it was now A-Number-One with me.

THE RAINBOW KERCHIEF AND THE FULL MOON

Jay Starre

Ricardo Sanchez grinned. He had an extremely accurate gaydar and he'd pegged the tall redheaded Sergeant Worth for a gay dude the moment he laid eyes on him. It had taken a lot of hinting around on Ricardo's part, telling the officer all kinds of intimate stuff without any real reaction, until just that morning his assumption was corroborated.

The platoon was dispatched to the California foothills for seven days of training maneuvers, housed in rudimentary tent barracks still hot from a late September heat wave. They were racing through an obstacle course of fences and ditches under an unusually hot autumn sun when a small group of them reached a towering wall covered with netting. A few moments of scuffling and milling around ensued as they jockeyed for turns at scaling the formidable obstacle. Ricardo turned to notice Sergeant Worth watching from the sidelines.

The sergeant held a kerchief, which he was swiping across his forehead to wipe away the sweat from the midday sun. For a moment, Ricardo just stared. The drill instructor was handsome as hell. He had pale-red eyebrows above pale-blue eyes and although his face was broad, his features were almost delicate, which made him look much younger than his nearly forty years. He wasn't given to smiling a heck of a lot, but he rarely frowned either. In fact, he always looked cool and collected. Nothing seemed to shake his equanimity.

The sergeant looked directly into Ricardo's eyes as he folded up the kerchief slowly and deliberately, clearly displaying the bright rainbow flag on the face of it. There was a simple pride to the way he made no effort to hide the gay symbol recognized the world over.

They had exchanged smiles, but then the sergeant's booming command rang out. "Climb that wall, Privates. Now!"

Afterward, the sweat of men who had driven themselves to exhaustion during the day's training session lingered in the air. Exhausted yet horny, most of them hoped to get a little sexual relief wherever they could—if the opportunity came up. Sergeant Worth called Ricardo aside to congratulate him on completing the course well ahead of anyone else. No one else was within earshot.

"I've got something to tell you about one of the other men, Sarge. I have a feeling you can help him figure out how to handle a problem he's got."

"What's the situation?"

"Danny's got a monster dick, Sarge. A really, really big one. Problem is, anyone who gets a look at it wants it in their mouth or up their ass. No one even thinks of Danny's ass. And he tells me he needs a little action back there, real bad it seems. You won't tell anyone will you? I trust you, Sarge, or I wouldn't tell you this kind of stuff."

Sergeant Worth nodded quietly. "As a reward for your

performance today, perhaps you and your buddy Private Park would like to enjoy some private time tonight. I'll make sure Second Unit showers are off-limits to everyone else."

Ricardo nodded enthusiastically and grinned happily, although Sergeant Worth merely nodded and strode off to attend to other business.

There were two shower buildings at the camp. One was close to the tent barracks, the other was at the north end beside the mechanics area and truck depot. That night, Danny and Ricardo slipped away without being noticed as the others sprawled on their cots drifting off to well-deserved sleep. It was a long walk in the light of a brooding full moon, and the two privates had to be careful not to rouse anyone. They weren't exactly doing anything wrong—but they wanted some privacy and didn't want anyone following them.

The two friends, the bold Ricardo and the easygoing Danny, were strikingly dissimilar in every way. Ricardo was short and stocky, and as a Mexican-American he'd sprung from stock more Indian than Spanish. His looks reflected it. He was very dark with smooth hairless skin, deep-brown eyes, bold features and full red lips. His army buzz cut only emphasized his large head and broad face. He was handsome in a distinctly mascu-line way, while his lush mouth and dreamy dark eyes softened an otherwise rough aspect.

Danny towered over his friend. At six-four he was broad-shouldered and big boned. When standing still he looked like a lumbering giant, but that was an illusion. He'd played college basketball for two years before he quit school and joined the Army. He was surprisingly agile and quick on his feet. His light-brown hair was cut short too, which revealed giant ears and emphasized his long hawk nose. Like Ricardo he had amazing eyes, but his were brilliant blue. The fair-haired soldier also had a wide, pink-lipped mouth that was perennially set in a friendly smile.

"Sarge said we wouldn't be disturbed. And he knows his shit," Ricardo said to his buddy in a low voice as they climbed the steps to the entrance.

"Yeah, he's real cool."

Just before they entered the building, Ricardo glanced up one final time at the hovering moon. He liked to take chances, and this little excursion was just up his alley. But he had to admit, that full moon seemed to challenge him. Others might find it romantic; he found it thrilling. He grinned with expectation as he playfully slapped his pal on the butt and hurried him in before anyone could spot them.

After quickly stripping down, the two privates moved into the shower room where they took their time dawdling under the warm spray and reveling in the luxury of their privacy. That privacy meant it was possible to act on their pent-up desires if they wanted to, and from the looks of Danny's rising cock, Ricardo knew he was in luck.

The sight of Danny's incredible cock stiffening up to its enormous dimensions had Ricardo feeling his tight asshole quivering in deference to the power of that tool. For his part, Danny soaped up the monster whanger with both fists as he watched his fellow soldier's reaction out of the corners of his eyes.

Ricardo didn't disappoint. He sprang wood too. Danny gauged the size of his pal's boner with an appreciative eye, deciding that though the thick tool was definitely big, it couldn't compare to his own lengthy piece. Still, there was no question it would feel great up his hungry asshole.

Unfortunately, judging by the intense look of greed in his fellow soldier's eyes as he stared at the fair-haired private's giant poker, Danny had little hopes of turning Ricardo's thoughts from his big hard-on to his smooth, puckered hole.

The tall soldier's dick was a stupendous tool that rose up to full mast without any trouble and at a moment's notice. No wonder everyone wanted a piece of it—and hardly paid any attention to his ass. Yet that ass was equally remarkable. Twin mountains of smooth flesh, high and jutting out from a trim waist, met at a deep crack with a hairless pink hole buried between.

The pair faced each other with stiff dicks in hand under the shower spray. Ricardo grinned boldly and winked as he began to slowly pump his. Danny bit his lip and dared to follow his pal's lead. With both big fists he began to rub his own up and down.

"Use some soap. Show me how you jerk that monster."

Danny giggled nervously but did as he was asked. Ricardo lathered up his own darker hard-on and the two began a slow pump and grind. In moments they were stroking within inches of each other. What might have happened next was forestalled by the sudden appearance of an intruder.

Sergeant Worth loomed in the doorway. He took in the sight of the two soapy boners with a quick eye. He cracked a hint of a smile, but his voice was calm and unrelenting.

"You two look like you've still got some energy that needs direction. The shower floors and the latrines require a final scrub down. I want you hard at it now, before it gets too late."

"Right now, Sergeant? Naked, Sergeant?" Ricardo asked with a smirk.

That ghost of a smile grew a little more evident as he stared the smart-ass private directly in the eye. "Well, since you've come up with the idea, why not? Get to work, Privates. I'll be back to check on you in an hour."

With that he spun on his heels and disappeared from the

shower doorway. They heard him slam the door, then the rattle of the lock's bolt. Danny looked a little uncertain but Ricardo whooped it up as he snatched his naked friend's arm and literally dragged him into the outer room where the latrines were located.

"Get out the buckets and fill them with water. I'll get the soap, mops and scrub brushes. We better make this place sparkle, or Sergeant Worth will be kicking our sorry butts all the way back to our bunks," Ricardo ordered his uncertain companion.

"Sure, Ricardo. But I've never done this buck naked before."

"It will be a fucking blast. I promise we'll have some fun."

Although Danny was skeptical that cleaning latrines could be fun, it didn't take more than fifteen minutes before Ricardo's promise bore fruit. Danny was hard at work crawling around on the wet floor scrubbing enthusiastically, always one to give his all to any task. Entirely naked as he was, with his dog tags dangling from his chest, his large butt wriggled with sensual enticement. His enormous cock also dangled. Swaying between his huge thighs, it wasn't quite hard but swollen nonetheless.

Ricardo grinned. He knew what would get that cock stiff! He tossed aside the mop in his hands and promptly dropped down on all fours behind his buddy. He buried his dark face between the pale cheeks and started licking the deep crack.

Danny's reaction was ecstatic. "Oh my god, Ricardo! Yeah! Lick my butt! Lick my hole too! Please! I love it, man."

The ass-munching soldier had a plan. Not that he didn't like eating the smooth ass and hole, but he was more interested in getting that giant dick stiff so he could ride it! He reached between the soldier's thighs, and Danny obligingly splayed wide to allow access to the monster rod hanging there.

It swelled up to its full girth after a few pulls, then stiffened rock hard as soon as Ricardo's tongue began to probe his fellow soldier's quivering hole. He did his best to lather up the pouting orifice with tickling swipes and little stabs until it began to flower wide and allow him to shove his tongue deep. Danny grunted and squirmed, pumping his cock into Ricardo's fist and rubbing his hefty butt against the soldier's mouth and nose.

Ricardo sucked on his pal's hole with loud slurps as Danny moaned loudly between pleas for more tongue up the ass. Slobbering all over the big soldier's crack, he finally abandoned the wet slot and slid his mouth downward along the smooth crack. He found the dangling balls, as smooth as the crack and plump as lemons, then pulled back on the prize, that giant cock. He swallowed up half of it in one juicy gulp.

Danny groaned and shuddered all over. "Oh man! Oh fuck! I gotta have some of your dick too!"

With that said, the bigger soldier heaved backward and twisted around, in the process knocking over the bucket of soapy water beside them. They found themselves aligned head to toe and wriggling naked in the slippery suds.

On top, the shorter private wasted no time in settling over his buddy's face. He aimed his cock at Danny's gaping mouth and plunged right in. The soldier gurgled noisily as he attempted to swallow the dark meat down to the balls. Ricardo faced the humongous cock rearing up between Danny's thighs with grinning anticipation. Just before he swooped down over it, he paused, certain he heard the slight click of the outer door unlocking. He cocked his ears and listened, and even with the loud slurps and grunts his buddy was making as his cock slid into his throat, Ricardo could hear the creak of the door opening, then closing.

Sergeant Worth was back! Good. Ricardo planned on giving the handsome sergeant a real show. He was absolutely certain the tall redhead would appreciate it! And hopefully, he'd join in, although that possibility was a little iffy. Sergeant Worth was very professional and very serious. He might allow his men to engage in a little fun and games, but he was also likely to hold himself to higher standards.

Ricardo was determined to do his best, though. His bigger plan included not only his own satisfaction, but his sweet-hearted buddy's satisfaction too. That meant Danny had to get some cock up the ass. Would Sergeant Worth oblige in that department?

The young private dove down over his pal's flaming pink column, opening wide and swallowing the mushroom crown then slithering deeper to take in a good few inches of the wide shaft. It only got wider nearer the base, and Ricardo was hard put to get much more than three-quarters of it in his mouth and throat.

He faced the open doorway to the changing area. Sergeant Worth would be watching from there. Pretending not to, he stole a glance upward from his position sprawled over the big soldier on the floor and caught a glimpse of polished boots. He was right!

He slobbered loudly, allowing spit to dribble down the thick shaft and pool around the base. He held nothing back. At the same time, he drilled downward into Danny's gurgling throat with his thighs clamped around the soldier's face so he couldn't see Sarge watching from the doorway.

But he didn't intend on putting off the main objective. He wanted the monster cock that was now in his mouth to work its mammoth magic up his ass! His own cock was wet and warm inside Danny's pulsing throat and he was afraid he might shoot a load at any moment, especially with Sarge watching.

It was time. He'd already laid the groundwork and it was simple enough to rise off Danny's face, spin around and then shove the big soldier a few feet forward across the slippery floor. One of the sinks was just above and within easy reach. Straddling Danny, he reached up and grabbed the bottle of hand lotion he'd planted there a few minutes earlier.

He knew he'd need one hell of a lot of lubricant if he was going to sit down on that humongous cock. With Danny staring up at him with those bright blue eyes, he squirted a stream of the slippery cream all over the big private's pink boner then crammed it up between his brown buttcheeks, right against his snug asshole.

"Oh yeah! Oh hell yeah! What a monster!"

"Can you take it, Ricardo? I don't want to hurt you…oh man! Yeah, just like that! Your hole feels so warm and slippery around my cock…"

Ricardo couldn't answer. He was huffing and puffing with the effort it took to swallow the immense dickhead slowly burrowing past his crinkled butt rim and into the steamy depths of his hungry hole. It felt absolutely amazing. He had a tight hole and loved the feeling of getting it stretched. Danny's cock was definitely doing that!

The flared head popped inside. With a grunt, he began to ride the enormous shaft. Yet even with the overwhelming sensation of all that meat pumping into his eager slot, he didn't forget about his buddy.

He reached back and clasped Danny's beefy thighs behind the knees. He pulled them up and then pushed them forward as he continued to ride the giant cock. He knew Sergeant Worth was watching and wanted to give him a good view of the prize he hoped the sergeant intended on capturing—Danny's puckered soldier asshole!

The sergeant smiled in the darkness just beyond the doorway to the latrine. All was going exactly according to plan. Ricardo was fairly transparent in his motives and his actions. Ricardo rode his buddy's cock. His solid hips drove up and down as he emitted a string of enthusiastic grunts. His dark-brown soldier butt rose and fell faster and faster as he mumbled over and over how great it felt to have that huge cock up his hole.

The cream-coated pink column strained against the quivering brown hole, sliding into it farther and farther with every plunge of Ricardo's luscious buttcheeks. At the same time, Danny's pale ass was in full view, along with his own twitching hole, gaping and clamping with excitement as his pal massaged his fat cock with his slippery butthole.

Sergeant Worth was definitely getting a show—and if Ricardo was correct, he would definitely be appreciating it!

As Ricardo rode his pal's cock for all he was worth, he imagined what would be going through Sarge's head right now. The observing sergeant was waiting, biding his time until the moment was right. As a combat-experienced sergeant he would know it was important to get down and dirty with the men he commanded. Ricardo stifled a little laugh as he thought that. Kneeling on the sudsy floor wasn't exactly like mud in the field, but it was a symbol of what Sarge would be willing to do in order to share the burden of war!

Sarge would be taking his time to contemplate the battle ahead. How many times had he told his men to do just that? Hopefully the sergeant was planning on plundering Danny's pouting pink soldier asshole and plundering it good!

As a gay man, Ricardo knew the sergeant would have a special affection for his soldier boys, more than perhaps a sergeant of a different inclination might have. Time and again he'd proven to Ricardo and the other men that he was not like most drill sergeants. He was certainly tough enough, pushing the recruits under his care to their limits and sometimes beyond in his quest to mold them into the best soldiers possible. He raised his voice, just like other sergeants, capable of shouting across the training field or obstacle course loud enough for even the least attentive of the men to hear his commands. But he didn't swear or denigrate, nor did he threaten. He merely gave his commands and expected results. If you didn't follow orders, there were inevitable consequences, which he was fully capable of meting out with a calm finality.

Ricardo dared to turn around. He was there! He had already taken off his boots and was right now stripping off his pants. As the private craned his neck around and watched, off came his shirt and then he was striding forward into the fray clad only in his dog tags.

Tall and all lean muscle, he was formidable in his pale muscular glory, especially with a scimitar-like curved cock rearing out from his hips. It took only a few strides for him to reach the pair of soldiers writhing in the suds on the floor against the sinks.

Ricardo met the sergeant's eyes and grinned just as he knelt behind them. Sergeant Worth offered a hint of a smile as he snatched up the discarded bottle of hand lotion, squirted a gooey stream over his stiff cock and took aim. Private Park's hole was perfectly exposed as his pal held his thighs against his chest and his ass reared up off the sudsy floor.

Bold as ever, Ricardo blurted out the obvious. "Sarge! Are you going to fuck Private Park, Sergeant? He would certainly be obliged if you did, Sergeant!"

"I am going to fuck Private Park. And I am going to fuck him good. Meanwhile, I am counting on you to do your utmost to swallow up as much of his big fat soldier cock as humanly possible. Understand, Private?"

"Yes, Sergeant!"

Danny was speechless, his blue eyes wide and his pink mouth gaping as he felt the sergeant's cock meet his pouting hole and slowly begin to slither inward. The head was bullet-shaped and perfect for opening up his tender slot without hurting. The steel-hard girth of the curved shaft that followed was like a heated missile slowly penetrating his defenses, and the young soldier totally capitulated.

The sergeant felt the private's asshole relaxing and then pushing out to swallow him. There was no doubting the surrender. He leaned forward and wrapped his arms around the humping Private Sanchez and held him as he steadily pumped his cock deeper and deeper into Private Park's warm and willing soldier hole.

The unexpected and longed for penetration had Danny in groaning ecstasy. Ricardo was happy as hell as he recognized that look on his pal's face. A cock up the ass was what he'd been needing from the first day he arrived at training camp. A barracks full of other young, randy soldiers had been almost too much to abide. Now, finally, he was getting fucked!

With the stimulus of that hard rod slowly gutting him, he began to thrust upward into Ricardo's ass. The dark private squealed aloud as another few inches of mammoth cock gored him. He loved it!

Together, the pair of privates rode cock, squirming, grunting and begging as the smiling sergeant steadily pounded the plump white can and squishy pink hole of one soldier and held on to the muscular body of the other as he writhed around his pal's monster meat.

The sudsy floor, the cream-coated cocks and holes, the sweaty muscular bodies, the cries of pleasure, all melded into a steamy, thrilling fuck-fest of soldier satisfaction. They worked in tandem, the sergeant plunging into the private's hole, which in turn forced the private's cock to drive upward into his fellow soldier's straining hole. Their coordination was superb, and all three became as one.

Pink cocks rammed willing holes as three soldiers writhed their way to a perfectly matched orgasm. In a show of timing rarely accomplished, one ejaculation followed the other as first Private Sanchez emitted a spray of goo high in the air, followed by Sergeant Worth slamming home up Private Park's hole to shoot a river of spunk, which precipitated the fair-haired soldier's own release, a spew of nut cream filling his buddy's quivering, dark, ass-channel.

They collapsed together in a naked pile on the sudsy floor, leaking cum and gasping for breath. Ricardo recognized the bemused look on his naïve pal's face that showed him to be completely surprised by the inexplicable turn of events. But he was sure the tall soldier had been more thoroughly satisfied than ever before. Ricardo smugly believed he'd been the manipulator behind the happy games they'd enjoyed and was more than pleased to see the wide grin on his buddy's satiated face.

A glance at Sergeant Worth told a similar tale. He was obviously well satisfied too. Yet Ricardo knew the sergeant was smarter than that, smarter than any private who believed he could turn the sergeant's good nature to his advantage. Sergeant Worth would certainly recognize the truth.

Fate had brought them together. A fortunate combination, the end of the ludicrous Don't Ask, Don't Tell policy, the careful use of a rainbow kerchief and the scattering of inhibitions under the influence of a round, full moon had all aided them in their effort.

So for Ricardo it was mission accomplished, the supreme result every soldier worked for. Maybe someday he'd become a drill instructor too, maybe one just half as good as Sergeant Worth!

ABOUT THE AUTHORS

SHANE ALLISON is the editor of *Hot Cops, Frat Boys, Brief Encounters, Middle Men, Cruising, Straight Guys* and the Gaybie Award–winning *College Boys*. His stories have graced the pages of *Surfer Boys, Beach Bums, Best Gay Erotica, Best Black Gay Erotica* and many more. He is at work on new stories and a novel.

Born in Los Angeles, **BEARMUFFIN** lives in San Diego where he enjoys watching the local surfers, sailors and Marines that inspire his erotic stories. You'll find his work in the gay anthologies *Sexy Sailors, Straight Guys* and *Cruising*.

MICHAEL BRACKEN's short fiction has been published in *Best Gay Romance 2010, Beautiful Boys, Biker Boys, Black Fire, Boy Fun, Boys Getting Ahead, Country Boys, Freshmen, The Handsome Prince, Homo Thugs, Hot Blood, The Mammoth Book of Best New Erotica 4, Men, Muscle Men, Teammates* and many other anthologies and periodicals.

JULIAN MARK is the "out" alter ego of a best-selling mystery writer. Julian's books include *Little Boy Lavender, Midtown Queen, Bath Boy, Shoretown, Games of Summer, Bummer Boy, Special Duty* and *Jump Squad*. His mystery author persona is, of course, a mystery.

AARON MICHAELS (aaron-michaels.com) is a romantic at heart. When he's not writing, he's watching way too much television and too many movies, which means his video game skills have pretty much fallen by the wayside. He is the author of the popular *Wiseguys* series.

EMILY MORETON published her first short story in 2007, for a charity anthology in aid of victims of Hurricane Katrina. Since then, she has continued to publish erotic short fiction regularly with a number of American publishers, including a story in *Heiresses of Russ 2012: The Year's Best Speculative Lesbian Fiction*.

GREGORY L. NORRIS (gregorylnorris.blogspot.com) lives and writes at the outer limits of New Hampshire and is the author of numerous books, including *The Q Guide to Buffy the Vampire Slayer* (Alyson Books) and *The Fierce and Unforgiving Muse: Thirteen Tales from the Terrifying Mind of Gregory L. Norris* (Evil Jester Press).

ROB ROSEN (therobrosen.com), author of the novels *Sparkle: The Queerest Book You'll Ever Love, Divas Las Vegas, Hot Lava, Southern Fried, Queerwolf* and *Vamp*, and editor of the anthology *Lust in Time: Erotic Romance through the Ages*, has had short stories featured in more than 170 anthologies.

DOMINIC SANTI (dominicsanti@yahoo.com) is a former technical editor turned rogue whose smutty stories have appeared in dozens of anthologies, including *Wild Boys*, *Hot Daddies*, *Country Boys*, *Uniforms Unzipped*, *Beach Bums*, *Gay Quickies*, *Sexy Sailors*, *Middle Men* and several volumes of *Best Gay Erotica*. Plans include an even dirtier historical novel.

Residing on English Bay in Vancouver, Canada, **JAY STARRE** pumps out erotic fiction for gay men's anthologies and websites. He is the author of two historical erotic novels. You can always check him out on Facebook.

DIRK STRONG has published erotic short stories in numerous anthologies, most recently in *College Boys*. His day job is in construction management.

LOGAN ZACHARY (loganzacharydicklit.com) lives in Minneapolis. *Calendar Boys* is a collection of his short stories. He has over a hundred erotic stories in print. His new erotic mystery, *Big Bad Wolf*, is a werewolf story set in Northern Minnesota.

ABOUT
THE EDITOR

NEIL PLAKCY (mahubooks.com) is the author of nineteen novels and collections of short stories, as well as the editor of many anthologies for Cleis Press, including *Hard Hats, Surfer Boys, Skater Boys, The Handsome Prince, Model Men, Sexy Sailors* and *Beach Bums*. He began his erotic writing career with a story for *Honcho* magazine called "The Cop Who Caught Me," and he's been writing about cops and sex ever since, most recently with seven novels in the *Mahu* mystery series. He lives in South Florida.

More from Neil Plakcy

Buy 4 books,
Get 1 *FREE**

The Handsome Prince
Gay Erotic Romance
Edited by Neil Plakcy

The Handsome Prince is a bawdy collection of bedtime stories brimming with classic fairy tale characters, reimagined and recast for any man who has dreamt of the day his prince will come. Masterfully edited by Neil Plakcy, these sexy stories fuel fantasies and remind us all of the power of true romance.
ISBN 978-1-57344-659-4 $14.95

Model Men
Gay Erotic Stories
Edited by Neil Plakcy

Ever wanted to reach into the pages of a fashion mag and pull out the guy of your dreams? *Model Men* features beautiful hunks and chiseled studs eager to jump off the page and right into your bed!
ISBN 978-1-57344-726-3 $14.95

Skater Boys
Gay Erotic Stories
Edited by Neil Plakcy

Easygoing, cocksure, and always willing to put their bodies on the line, skaters are living paragons of desire. Between the pages of *Skater Boys*, you'll find sexy athletes who redefine *extreme sports* in the hottest ways you can imagine.
ISBN 978-1-57344-401-9 $14.95

Hard Hats
Gay Erotic Stories
Edited by Neil Plakcy

What is it about a hot guy with a tool belt? With their natural brand of macho, the sheen of honest sweat on flesh, and the enticements of hammers and pneumatic drills, men with tool belts rank among the hottest icons in gay erotic fantasy.
ISBN 978-1-57344-312-8 $14.95

Surfer Boys
Gay Erotic Stories
Edited by Neil Plakcy

Is it any wonder that surfers fuel sexual fantasies the world over? All that exposed, sun-kissed skin, those broad shoulders and yearning for adventure make a stud on a surfboard irresistible. Get ready for a long, hard ride.
ISBN 978-1-57344-349-4 $14.95

The Best in Gay Romance

Best Gay Romance 2014
Edited by Timothy Lambert and R. D. Cochrane

The best part of romance is what might happen next...that pivotal moment where we stop and realize, *This is wonderful*. But most of all, love—whether new or lifelong—creates endless possibilities. *Best Gay Romance 2014* reminds us all of how love changes us for the better.
ISBN 978-1-62778-011-7 $15.95

The Handsome Prince
Gay Erotic Romance
Edited by Neil Plakcy

In this one and only gay erotic fairy tale anthology, your prince will come—and come again!
ISBN 978-1-57344-659-4 $14.95

Afternoon Pleasures
Erotica for Gay Couples
Edited by Shane Allison

Filled with romance, passion and lots of lust, *Afternoon Pleasures* is irresistibly erotic yet celebrates the coming together of souls as well as bodies.
ISBN 978-1-57344-658-7 $14.95

Fool for Love
New Gay Fiction
Edited by Timothy Lambert and R. D. Cochrane

For anyone who believes that love has left the building, here is an exhilarating collection of new gay fiction designed to reignite your belief in the power of romance.
ISBN 978-1-57344-339-5 $14.95

Boy Crazy
Coming Out Erotica
Edited by Richard Labonté

Editor Richard Labonté's unique collection of coming-out tales celebrates first-time lust, first-time falling into bed, and first discovery of love.
ISBN 978-1-57344-351-7 $14.95

Men on the Make

Get Under the Covers
with These Hunks

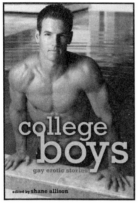

Rousing, Arousing
Adventures with Hot Hunks

The Riddle of the Sands
By Geoffrey Knight

Will Professor Fathom's team of gay adventure-hunters uncover the legendary Riddle of the Sands in time to save one
of their own? Is the Riddle a myth, a mirage or the greatest
engineering feat in the history of ancient Egypt?
"A thrill-a-page romp, a rousing, arousing
adventure for queer boys-at-heart men."
—Richard Labonté, Book Marks
ISBN 978-1-57344-366-1 $14.95

Divas Las Vegas
By Rob Rosen

Filled with action and suspense, hunky
blackjack dealers, divine drag queens,
strange sex and sex in strange places, plus a
Federal agent or two, *Divas Las Vegas* puts
the sin in Sin City.
ISBN 978-1-57344-369-2 $14.95

The Back Passage
By James Lear

Blackmail, police corruption, a dizzying
network of spy holes and secret passages,
and a nonstop queer orgy backstairs and
everyplace else mark this hilariously hard-
core mystery by a major new talent.
ISBN 978-1-57344-243-5 $13.95

The Secret Tunnel
By James Lear

"Lear's prose is vibrant and colourful.... This
isn't porn accompanied by a wah-wah gui-
tar, this is porn to the strains of Beethoven's
Ode to Joy, each vividly realised ejaculation
accompanied by a fanfare and the crashing
of cymbals."—*Time Out London*
ISBN 978-1-57344-329-6 $15.95

A Sticky End
A Mitch Mitchell Mystery
By James Lear

To absolve his best friend and sometimes
lover from murder charges, Mitch races
around London finding clues while bed-
ding the many men eager to lend a hand—
or more.
ISBN 978-1-57344-395-1 $14.95

Best Erotica Series

"Gets racier every year."—*San Francisco Bay Guardian*

Buy 4 books, Get 1 FREE*

Best Women's Erotica 2014
Edited by Violet Blue
ISBN 978-1-62778-003-2 $15.95

Best Women's Erotica 2013
Edited by Violet Blue
ISBN 978-1-57344-898-7 $15.95

Best Women's Erotica 2012
Edited by Violet Blue
ISBN 978-1-57344-755-3 $15.95

Best Bondage Erotica 2014
Edited by Rachel Kramer Bussell
ISBN 978-1-62778-012-4 $15.95

Best Bondage Erotica 2013
Edited by Rachel Kramer Bussel
ISBN 978-1-57344-897-0 $15.95

Best Bondage Erotica 2012
Edited by Rachel Kramer Bussel
ISBN 978-1-57344-754-6 $15.95

Best Lesbian Erotica 2014
Edited by Kathleen Warnock
ISBN 978-1-62778-002-5 $15.95

Best Lesbian Erotica 2013
Edited by Kathleen Warnock
Selected and introduced by
Jewelle Gomez
ISBN 978-1-57344-896-3 $15.95

Best Lesbian Erotica 2012
Edited by Kathleen Warnock
Selected and introduced by
Sinclair Sexsmith
ISBN 978-1-57344-752-2 $15.95

Best Gay Erotica 2014
Edited by Larry Duplechan
Selected and introduced by Joe Manetti
ISBN 978-1-62778-001-8 $15.95

Best Gay Erotica 2013
Edited by Richard Labonté
Selected and introduced by Paul Russell
ISBN 978-1-57344-895-6 $15.95

Best Gay Erotica 2012
Edited by Richard Labonté
Selected and introduced by
Larry Duplechan
ISBN 978-1-57344-753-9 $15.95

Best Fetish Erotica
Edited by Cara Bruce
ISBN 978-1-57344-355-5 $15.95

Best Bisexual Women's Erotica
Edited by Cara Bruce
ISBN 978-1-57344-320-3 $15.95

Best Lesbian Bondage Erotica
Edited by Tristan Taormino
ISBN 978-1-57344-287-9 $16.95

* Free book of equal or lesser value. Shipping and applicable sales tax extra.
Cleis Press • (800) 780-2279 • orders@cleispress.com
www.cleispress.com

Ordering is easy! Call us toll free or fax us to place your MC/VISA order.
You can also mail the order form below with payment to:
Cleis Press, 2246 Sixth St., Berkeley, CA 94710.

ORDER FORM

QTY	TITLE	PRICE
_____	_____	_____
_____	_____	_____
_____	_____	_____
_____	_____	_____
_____	_____	_____
_____	_____	_____
_____	_____	_____
_____	_____	_____

SUBTOTAL _____

SHIPPING _____

SALES TAX _____

TOTAL _____

Add $3.95 postage/handling for the first book ordered and $1.00 for each additional book. Outside North America, please contact us for shipping rates. California residents add 9% sales tax. Payment in U.S. dollars only.

* Free book of equal or lesser value. Shipping and applicable sales tax extra.

Cleis Press • Phone: (800) 780-2279 • Fax: (510) 845-8001
orders@cleispress.com • www.cleispress.com
You'll find more great books on our website

Follow us on Twitter @cleispress • Friend/fan us on Facebook